NORTHERN STORIES
1988

*Edited by Kitty Fitzgerald, John Ward
& John Killick*

GW00702769

LITTLEWOOD PRESS
THE NANHOLME CENTRE
Shaw Wood Road
Todmorden
Lancs

Stories: © Various Authors 1988
Cover Illustration: © Stephen Pickles 1988
ISBN 0 946407 42 8

Published by the Littlewood Press, The Nanholme Centre,
Shaw Wood Road, Todmorden, Lancs
Printed at the Arc and Throstle Press, Todmorden
Typeset by Bryan Williamson, Manchester

CONTENTS

Preface by John Killick 7

P.C. *Keith* The Cock-Eyed Nail 9
John Latham Licket 13
Alison Guinane Morning 18
Nancy Clare Wynne On Such A Bed As This 23
David Craig The Perfect Place 29
Mick North P.S. Billy Pinch 35
Carol Barker Outside In 40
Pat Bince Tarzan's Mate 45
Robert Forster Adjudicator 49
Valerie Smith The Veil 56
Graham Mort Mud Bastard 61
Theresa Tomlinson The Oakum Room 68
Neil Roberts The Wedding March 71
Peter Ryde Going For Walks With Johnno 77
Sue Wilsea End Of The World 84
Chris Firth Justice 87
M. Aslett Heaven And The Have Nots 94
Alison McLeod Simon S.S. Says 100
Arthur Appleton The English Maradonna 107
Irene Rawnsley A Cold Morning 113
Joan Thornton The Wedding 119
David Almond Nesting 128
Barry Mathias Observations From An Outside Toilet 137
Dorothy Nimmo Landscape With Nude Figures 141

About The Authors 149

PREFACE

This Anthology is the product of a Competition organized by the Littlewood Press in the early months of 1988. Entries were invited from authors resident in the areas covered by the five Northern Regional Arts Associations in England. There was a limitation on length of 3,500 words, but none on subject-matter. The Competition attracted 408 entries. The Judges were Kitty Fitzgerald, John Ward and John Killick. The winners were presented with cheques by Stan Barstow at an event held at Calderdale Central Library, Halifax on 20th October. Prizes were awarded as follows: FIRST: 'Nesting' by David Almond; SECOND: (shared): 'Landscape With Nude Figures' by Dorothy Nimmo; 'Mud Bastard' by Graham Mort; THIRD: 'Justice' by Chris Firth.

The Judges were agreed that, though few outstanding stories surfaced, the general level of the best entries was such that the production of an Anthology was highly desirable. There was little argument about which stories to include; we believe that the variety and liveliness of the contents of this book fully justify all the work that has gone into its compilation. We were careful to exclude all stories which did not conform to the rules of the Competition: one excellent story, which would otherwise have been a prizewinner, is omitted for this reason. We decided not to include more than one story by any author so as to widen the representation of the region's writers: John Latham, Dorothy Nimmo, Alison Guinane and Robert Forster would otherwise have been further represented. The contents of this book is very much a 'committee' decision: we did not include anything that did not command the assent of all three Judges.

We are sure that this Anthology fills a gap in the Northern publishing scene, and hope that sales will be such as to encourage the establishment of the Competition as a Biennial event.

JOHN KILLICK

The Cock-Eyed Nail

Almost as soon as he'd married her, she wondered why he had. They made love of a sort once a week, but never on Fridays because of football on Saturdays. Sometimes there'd be a binge of sex which left her puzzled. She could see it in the mirror in the mornings. It went with some cycle in him. She just happened to be handy.

For a long time she loved him – through his getting fatter, so his belly came in the door first; through the slow discolouring of his teeth where the lower lip hung away from them. He had a slack mouth until he sneered.

She'd found his sneer exciting as long as she felt it was them against the rest. But the sneers took a separate turn. If she agreed with him, he'd stop her in mid-sentence: "I don't see as how it can matter to you." And she'd go away and be busy in the kitchen.

He was careful not to be too hard on her – he never hit her. He just didn't show her any love. He let her look after him but he didn't want her dog-eyed fondness. He'd frown or turn his head away and she'd know she'd done it again – irritated him. He didn't stop her bringing him his slippers.

It all came to settle – the aggravation – on that nail. Next to the big toe on her left foot. He took to making remarks about it. "Can't you cut it so it's level? It's all skew-whiff."

She tried. But then it wasn't level with itself. The white edge was thick at one end and nearly disappeared at the other. She'd have painted her nails but he thought that was the sign of a slut. She didn't mention his teeth.

It meant that sandals were out – and she liked the feel of bare legs on hot days. She kept her tights on – to stop the way his eyes would slide down to that toe. But he stared at the point where it was – as if he had x-ray eyes.

She tried to work it out: the nail was square with itself; the root was wrong. Tipped out of true. Maybe someone could make it right. The doctor said, "Does it hurt?"

"No, Doctor."

"Well, then! Nothing to worry about, is there?" She couldn't bring herself to say.

He came near to hitting her for going to the doctor. All he said was, "You want your head examined." She bought some heavy shoes.

It turned out they weren't heavy enough. One day she tried to get the old treadle-machine upstairs. Mrs Barnes' lad from next-door-but-two helped her.

"My husband doesn't like things upset," she explained to Mrs Barnes. "He'll make a big thing out of it if I wait and ask him."

"Some folk get things all their own road", Mrs Barnes said, but lent her Fred.

It was more awkward than she'd thought. His mother had always had the old Singer downstairs, covered in potted plants; now she wanted the space.

"Open that door", she told Fred. "It'll have to go out and in again. Never get it round without."

By the time she'd realized he was going up first, it was too late — anyway, he wasn't any bigger than she was. They were mangaging till he trapped his hand on the bannister and let go. She held the cast-iron push of it for a long second or two before her foot slipped. She pressed back against the wall as the whole thing slid down. As it went, her left foot took the full weight. The cock-eyed nail caught the iron castor on its root.

The machine jolted down from step to step. It carried on out the open door and across the street, falling over on its side as it hit the opposite kerb outside Mrs Dearden's. Fred shot off home. She sat down heavily on the stairs.

His shape was suddenly black in the doorway. He must have been coming up the street — seen the Barnes lad doing a bunk, Mrs Dearden's open mouth at the machine outside her front. Other doors had opened. She could see faces staring from behind him. Mrs Howarth's began to say "Eh, love, what can I...?" He closed the door as if he hadn't heard.

"We'll have them all round. Just at tea-time. Which foot is it?"

She didn't answer. He could see where she was holding it. He went out again to phone for the doctor.

For days she could feel all her toes stuck off the end of her foot like sausages under the bandage. When the swelling had gone down, it was the funny nail that came off. "Maybe it'll grow straight now," she thought.

He helped her more while she was hobbling about. Then, she showed him the toe with the nail gone. She saw the sneer:

"That's a right mess, and no mistake."

"There's a chance it'll grow back straight."

He didn't notice the dog-eyed look go out of her eyes — he'd gone in the bathroom when it faded.

While she waited for the nail to grow up, she began to realise: it wasn't the cock-eyed nail — it was her. It wouldn't matter which way it grew — he'd never be any different. She discovered she wasn't upset.

She didn't say anything to him. She carried on working it out in her head while she watched for the nail to grow. It didn't. That toe stayed blank-looking. When spring came, she took off her heavy shoes and fished out her old sandals from under the bed. She left her tights off.

When he came home from work, she was sitting on the front door-step in the sun. He stood in front of her in his work-clothes, the leather belt holding his belly up. His teeth were getting worse. He was looking at the toe.

"You've got your shoes off", he said.

"Yes, I have. They're my feet." Her tone made him look at her face. She was watching his. It was a shock – they'd spent years watching while the other wasn't looking, registering reactions from the corner of the eye. Now their eyes held, couldn't glance off.

"You won't have to put up with this toe – nail or no nail – for much longer. By tomorrow night, I'll be staying at our Joan's place."

He stood there, the slack mouth expressionless.

"And if you're wondering what brought this on – it's just time, that's all. I'm going to help her in the shop – and the room at the back has a sink. There's a toilet in the yard – till I've found somewhere proper. It'll do me."

"Suit yourself."

He didn't argue about it. They spent the next day just as if she wasn't going. It didn't seem to bother either of them and she wondered why she hadn't gone before. Not as if there were kids to consider. Still, better late than never.

Sometimes, when she was serving in the shop, she'd see him go past at dinner-time. Once or twice he even came in for a packet of biscuits or some cigarettes. It was one of those all-sorts shops. Hot pies at dinner-time – but he'd never liked shop-bought pies. When he paid her, he kept his eyes down, counting it out. But then he did that with anybody.

Years later, when the divorce was through, she was living in a two-up, two-down in Henry Street. She and another woman shared the rent. It worked out very convenient.

She had to smile when she heard he'd got married again. Joan had seen them on New Street: "He's just as fat, if not more. And you'd never credit it..." She paused.

"Well?"

"She's got a club foot."

The smile broadened. She giggled.

"It's nothing to laugh at!" Joan said. Our Edith's cousin was at school with her. Right strong-minded she is. She's not one to let it get her down!"

"Poor bugger," was all she said.

Joan couldn't tell from that smile — which one she meant.

John Latham

Licket

Ernest idolised me. He often brought me cold toast wrapped in newspaper to school. Crusty, thickly buttered, it tasted gorgeous — its flavour heightened by Ernest's face, rocking, sometimes slavering, ecstatic, just a few inches below me. Ernest, when he stood up straight, was tall, but he almost always crouched, as though expecting blows. As though inviting them, in fact. Sometimes I felt compelled to thump him. When that happened he didn't protect himself. He just crouched lower, looked imploringly at me, his eyes glistening with tears. I didn't thump him often, or hard, because I liked him. More importantly, in some way I didn't understand, I feared him, even worshipped him. He had a gentleness, a meekness that was phenomenally strong.

Once Johnnie rubbed mud into his face so he couldn't see. He stood there in the playground, arms loose-dangling, out of balance, blind eyes searching for the sun. Johnnie would push him over, with just one finger, gently to the centre of his forehead. But he'd clamber up again, crouching lower than before, head craned back, still scanning. He made no sound. We stood round him in a circle, laughing until we cried. He was not a boy, but some stranded creature from the past.

As time went on, he took longer and longer to regain his feet, and he was crouching so low that his chin was almost scraping the tarmac. Johnnie seemed only to have to point his finger for Ernest to collapse. Slowly we grew quiet, ashamed, though no-one protested or went away. Eventually Yonner, the greatest fighter in the school, held up his hand, and Johnnie had to stop. "Take him to the washroom and clean that mud away", he ordered. And Johnnie had to. He hated Ernest after that.

Ernest's mother was tall and sad, with a faraway smile. Usually she brought him to school – even when he was ten – and was waiting for him at the end of the day. In between, she scrubbed and cleaned at the big sandstone house at the furthest side of Kingsley hill. She would stand at the gate, holding the green railings, oblivious to the hordes of children rushing, pushing past her. Her eyes were fixed on the door through which Ernest, always last, eventually came. A wicker basket dangled from her arm. It held straw and Ernest's cat. He always carried it to school and back again, at times lifting the lid and speaking softly into it. When it was raining his mother brought an oil-skin cape, which he took the basket inside, his head hidden, a lumpy tent. Then, his mother had to steer him down the road.

One day Mrs Moon invited me to their house to play with him. I was curious to see how they lived, and since Johnnie didn't know about the arrangement, I went. The cottage was tiny, but unlike Phil's it was clean and orderly. It was heated by an iron stove on which she cooked, and when she lit the oil-lamps, throwing yellow pools of light on to the low ceiling, I felt cosy and close to Ernest. This feeling was heightened when the wind stirred the flames and the pools wobbled for a while.

Ernest was more confient, more fluent than at school, where he scarcely spoke at all, and was always bottom of the class. He didn't crouch as much. He took my arm and drew me to the dresser, pointing to a dark and somewhat out-of-focus photograph of an awkward-looking man in uniform. He had the same vague smile as Ernest when he stared out of the window during sums. "My dad", he said. "He was killed when I was none. Look at the shiny buckle on his belt". I did. It was gleaming, but not as much as Ernest's eyes as he pointed out the details on the photograph, never touching it.

His mother was baking oat-cakes on the stove, and their wonderful smell made me curl and crisp inside. While we were waiting for them to brown Ernest brought me a wooden box with a sliding lid. "Do you want to see my darlins?", he asked. "Your what?" "My darlins. My darlins made of plasticine". "Yep". I replied.

Ernest was always playing with plasticine at school. He carried a great multi-coloured ball of it in his pocket, and was forever moulding, pinching it, drawing it out into fine whorled threads, dextrously spiralling them down into a cone. He smelled of plasticine.

Proudly he drew open the lid. Inside the box were groups of figurines, tiny, delicately wrought. A few were monochrome but most were in a mixture of subtly blended colours. He lifted some out so I could see them better. Most possessed a human shape, but were deformed in such a way as to make me understand what they were feeling. They disturbed me.

"This is 'Glum' " said Ernest, pointing. "This is 'Frighten'. This is 'Scrape' ". He lifted another one towards me, very gently. It was female, largely purple and green, neck twisted to the side, body arched backwards so the stomach was stretched and hollow. "This is 'Agony' ", he said. I daren't touch it. "All these are my darlins. I change them but they never go away". I was trying not to tremble. "Great", I said. Ernest seemed alight, apart.

I think his mother had been watching and understood my fear. "Show him 'Licket' ", she called. "And then the oatcakes will be done". He came slowly from his trance, drew a larger figure from the box. It was a boy, plump, in stripes of yellow and red. I whistled. There was no mistaking it. The buttocks were deliberately too large, the pigeon-toes were more twisted than normal, but the mirthless smile was that of Johnnie Greenaway. I grinned. My nervousness had passed away. "This is 'Licket'", he said. "Watch".

He fetched a tin of syrup from the kitchen, removed the lid, and holding Licket by his feet, dipped him in. Then he placed him upright on a saucer, and called the cat with a faint shushing sound. The cat padded over and delicately tongued a glob of syrup from Licket's nose. I started laughing. Ernest gripped my arm. "Laugh inside you", he whispered. "Not waste your stomach".

For the next five minutes or so the cat fastidiously licked the syrup away: under the chin, around the belly, between the thighs. When it came to the feet it placed a paw gently on the figure's head and rocked it this way and that, so its tongue could slide underneath. Eventually it finished and strolled away. Licket was bone-dry. I felt that Johnnie had been raped. It had been very funny, but I felt uneasy.

"Time for oat-cakes!", Ernest's mother called. They were piping hot, served with a pitcher of spring water. We cleared the plate, me eating most. They were delicious. Ernest's mother seemed pleased. "You must come again", she said. I nodded.

But I wasn't sure. In fact, I didn't think I would. The balance was too different in this cottage. Ernest didn't crouch, he wasn't deferential, and I'd been frightened by Agony. Had Ernest shown her to me knowing I'd be scared? I thought he probably had.

He came with me to the gate. Outside he seemed as gawky and unconfident as ever. "Tomorrow's a half-day," I whispered. "Why don't you bring some of your darlins to school? We'll go off to the quarry afterwards". He looked uncertain. "Bring some plasticine and you can show me how to make them". His face brightened. "But you'd better not tell your Mum". He nodded.

On the following afternoon I walked with Ernest up Silver Pin, on the way to the sandstone quarry. He was very excited, not saying much but smiling suddenly at me and skipping over tree-roots. He had a tin under his arm, which I supposed held some of his darlins. Near the snake-tree he halted, fished an oat-cake from his pocket, shyly handed it to me. It smelled of plasticine, but tasted good. Ernest looked proud, infinitely vulnerable. I felt nervous and ashamed. What Ernest didn't know was that Johnnie was waiting for us in the quarry. I'd told him about the darlins – though not 'Licket' – that morning, at school, and Johnnie said we'd have some fun.

As we descended the steep trail through rain-heavy ferns into the quarry, a curl of smoke rose from the cleft in the inward-leaning sandstone face, where Johnnie and I sometimes cooked on Saturdays. He was squatting by the fire, feeding logs into the space below the metal grille. He heard us, turned and rose. "Howdy, Ernest", he called. "Brought your darlins?" He was grinning just like Licket. Ernest looked towards me, part reproachfully, part in supplication, and clutched his tin more tightly. "It's O.K.", I said. "He just wants to look at them". I reached out slowly for the tin, so that Johnnie could see I wanted him to treat the darlins gently. Ernest recoiled, then handed it over, quietly.

Johnny snatched the tin, plonked it on the ground, swiftly opened the lid. His eyes widened. He was silent for a while. Ernest was sucking his thumb. Johnnie took one out, held it to the light. I saw orange and blue hoops around the figure's chest. I thought it might be 'Scrape'. "Pretty good", he said. "Terrific!" He turned to Ernest, who was watching him with large, sad eyes. "They're great, Ernest. But they're cold". He shook Scrape quickly to and fro. "See him shivering. We'll have to warm him up".

Ernest looked imploringly at me, and then the tin. I followed his gaze and saw the stretched abandonment of Agony, in emerald and violet, her colours lighter in the afternoon sun than in his cottage. "I think the sunlight will soon warm them", I said to Johnnie. "Did-dums babbies wrap-ups?", he replied softly, his contempt scarcely veiled, completely confident of his power over me.

Johnnie fascinated me. I sought him out. I trembled at his voice and especially his touch. I was in love with him, and he knew it. He used this knowledge with great finesse. He didn't care about me. Suddenly, I hated Ernest for coming between us. "They'll be better on the fire", I said, but when Ernest flinched I added "We'll only warm them up a bit".

I arranged the figures on the blackened metal tray we used for frying eggs. They balanced perfectly. Ernest was crouching beside me, rocking. Johnnie slid the tray onto the grille. One fell over, but he swiftly picked it up, pressed it gently into place.

The fire was subdued, just a few logs glowing. The sun was shafting into the quarry, throwing shadows of the figures on the sandstone wall behind them. They were as grave and deformed as the originals. There was something holy in their passive stillness and Ernest's silent rocking. "Are they warm yet, Johnnie?", I asked, trying to make my voice sound neutral. He hesitated, then when Ernest tensed he shook his head.

A sweet aroma was rising from the tray. Agony's feet were weeping. Then one figure sagged at the knees, crumpled to the tray. A bubble swelled and burst at the base of another. Where they touched the metal they were turning black. All of them were slowly sinking.

"Don't hell my darlings!" Ernest screamed, and lunged forwards. Johnnie swiped him with his wrist. He toppled back onto the cold sand, always in shadow at the foot of the cliff. He screamed again. "Don't hell them. Please!" His voice echoed round the four walls of the quarry.

I was watching Agony. She had stretched so far backwards her head had touched the tray and was bubbling. Ernest was clutching my arm. Then her stomach cleaved. She was slowly ripped apart into two pieces, solidifying as they flowed along the tray towards each other.

"They're warm now", Johnnie snapped, and strode off through the bracken without looking back. I used a pair of sticks to slide the tray onto the sand. There wasn't much that could be salvaged. The stench was sickening. Ernest cried "My darlins helled to death!". He grabbed the trunk of Agony, stuffed it in his mouth. I could feel the pain sweep through him, but his teeth were clamped. He wouldn't let go. He swallowed.

I moved towards him, but his eyes avoided me. He lifted the tray up to the fire, and with a broken slate scraped the remains of the last of the figures onto the smouldering logs. They were mostly black, just a touch of colour here and there. He raked ash over them, took his tin and rose. Once more, he wouldn't meet my eye. He was tall again, and as he climbed up the track to leave the quarry the sun struck his yellow hair and made it blaze.

Morning

It was autumn again, and savage gusts drove the dried carcasses of leaves against the side of the house, where they scraped like desparate fingernails on the good stock brick. From her bed, Maureen could just lean over the sill to gaze at the neat suburban garden, now awash with torn scraps of burnt rags that were once chrysanthemums. Bright red dahlia petals were strewn, bleeding, over the lawn, and a few panic-stricken leaves clung to the dark outline of her stags-horn tree. Last week it had flamed orange and vermilion; today its long, writhing branches clawed upwards viciously in the soft, October sun.

She dropped the curtain back into place and looked at the wristwatch lying on the bedside cabinet, where she had left it yesterday. Eight o'clock. Exactly twelve hours ago, then. There were voices downstairs, and her mother let someone in at the front door. She listened, trying to identify them, and hoped they wouldn't come upstairs. She didn't want to see anyone. She wanted to be alone, to nurse her great emptiness

"And how are you this morning, then, Mrs Maguire, my dear? Surely, it's a dreadful thing to happen, but there's them I know with a houseful, would think it a blessing from God!"

"Yes."

"Then again, it won't be long before you're after forgetting all this and starting another."

"No."

The freckled face, carefully compounded of common-sense and sympathy, turned away from Maureen towards the window, where just enough pale sunshine filtered through the floral curtains for her to inspect the thermometer. She sat on the edge of the bed, and kneaded Maureen's stomach.

"Any pain? No? That's good."

"My breasts hurt."

She felt foolish, like one of those caricatures on seaside postcards: flat stomach, huge ripe breasts thrusting out in front. Their fullness mocked the empty hollow in her womb, where the echo created absurdity out of her pain. She remembered reading about some boys who pumped air into toads, to see them burst, for fun, and felt a pang of horror, all over again.

The nurse snapped shut her black holdall and stood up, smoothing her uniform coat with one slim, capable hand and patting her neat, brown curls with the other. She twitched the creased cover where she had been sitting, and turned to go.

"I'll pop in tomorrow to see you again, my dear. Stay in bed until then, now won't you?"

"Yes."

She paused at the door, and for a moment her gaze rested uncomfortably on the empty cot against the far wall, its pink and blue covers carefully laid. Then she was gone.

Ten o'clock. Her mother appeared, with tea in a china cup and a biscuit. Usually it was a mug with her birthsign on. She sat up to drink it.

"I've an apple pie for later."

"Thanks. That'll be nice."

Last time her mother had worn her pale blue wedding outfit to visit her at the hospital, and presented her with a bunch of pink and white carnations whose scent mingled in her memory with Johnson's talc and nappies dried on the line. This time she had brought a lily in an earthenware pot, which hung its head in the corner.

Maureen's two-year-old daughter wandered in and stood fidgetting uncertainly with the fringe of her housecoat, lying across the bottom of the bed. She seemed quiet, subdued, intent on what she was doing. Maureen spoke softly to her, unable to forget the anguished screams behind her as they carried her into the ambulance yesterday. There was no sign now that the child remembered it. She must have presented a frightening and inconguous spectacle, lurching down the stairs in a carried wheelchair, daisy-strewn nightdress catching on rose thorns, as she passed prying curtains all along the path.

"You will eat some of the pie, won't you? Do you no good to starve. I'll cut some, ready."

"Yes. Thanks."

Mother had powdered her nose, but her eyes were very tired. They seemed wider than ever, very blue and inarticulate, as they stared awkwardly over the red rose on the tea-cup. The furrow between them deepened and she smiled unhappily through tight lips. Maureen remembered the warm, scented softness of the cheek brushing hers, years ago. Now her neck looked old and thin in the frill of her red chiffon blouse.

"Michael's out mowing the lawn...Best thing, really...to keep occupied..."

"My back's aching. I'll have to lie down."

Left alone, she listened to the rhythmical whirr of the mower and felt lulled by it. Everything inside was so still. A vaccuum. If she half closed her eyes, she could imagine she saw, through the blur, the small rounded form under its pink and blue knitted cover, rising and falling softly as it slept. The sun picked out the interwoven primroses and pansies on the curtains and invested the room with a sanctified glow. It shone on the fluted folds of the polished oak wardrobe, and brightened the silver crucifix above the hearth. It gleamed on the round, rain-washed coals of the rabbit's eyes in the baby's empty cot, and lingered on the ashes in the iron grate.

When Maureen was twelve, her white rabbit and her diary were thrown away. The rabbit was small and grubby, and didn't say anything; the diary had clearly said too much. The rabbit's eyes melted great, plastic tears over the crackling paper in the embers, while she watched. The old experiences somehow fused with the new, and onto the pyre would go the tiny, crumpled infant streaked with stained mucus which had curled pathetically on the delivery table.

She hated lying flat, but if she turned on her side her breasts hurt. She'd had to lie flat last night, floundering and gasping like a landed fish on the long, white slab, beneath probing angle lamps.

"You know this baby's dead, Mrs Maguire?"

"Yes."

"Right. Do you think you're ready to start pushing?"

Difficult, now, to lie still upstairs, while others carried on living. But once, as a child, she'd crept down to find gas seeping under the door of the living room, and her father, unconscious, on the floor. Next day, he'd gone outside and attacked the garden, burning lilac trees and rose trellis till all was bare. Then he'd planted dahlias...

Eleven thirty. She must have dozed, and a door slamming jolted her awake. There was a confusion of voices in the hall, sounding unnaturally loud and cheerful. She identified various relatives.

"We won't stay long...Don't want to be a nuisance..."

"Yes...We brought a little something...Cheer her up..."

"No...it is a long time, isn't it..."

"Births, marriages and deaths, eh?"

"Sh...sh...Come in and sit down."

They dropped to a hush and were suddenly muffled as the door closed on them. Occasionally, Michael's staccato laugh startled the coffined whispers beneath her. She turned her head and looked at the apple pie her mother had placed on the cabinet beside her. The crust, four inches deep and pale as a shroud, hugged its thin, white apple layers where the knife had cut. The sun had gone in, and an immense weariness drew her downwards. She turned her face to the wall and wished she could cry.

The doorbell rang, and the living room door released a crescendo of sound as someone went to answer it.

"Why, hello, Father!"

Inaudible reply.

"No,no, come in and have a bite to eat...Yes...Terrible...Such a shock...Never happened in our family before...Can't think..."

"Well, well. We all have our crosses."

A dry husk of anger hardened around the hollow where the embryo had been, and dispelled Maureen's weariness. A draught lifted the dust in the tiled hearth and a few, sharp raindrops punctuated the silence upstairs. The sun no longer warmed the grate. The primroses and pansies seemed blurred and lifeless. Her potted lily shone its speckled, ghostly sheen in the alcove and snaked its long tongue towards the cot. She threw back the duvet and gingerly edged herself out of bed. There were no stitches this time. It didn't even seem very sore. As if nothing had happened. She felt the looseness of her belly sag as she pulled herself upright against the chest of drawers. Drawers full of knitted baby things.

Her white and gold flowered nightdress was crumpled and a small bloodstain showed on the back. Embarassing. Marked out in her shame. How would she explain her empty arms?

"How's the baby?"

"What did you have, then? Boy or girl?"

"I lost it."

As if she had carelessly or wilfully mislaid it, like an umbrella, on the Tube. She could hear their confidential murmurs and feel their looks of pity following her home from the shops.

There was a clatter of cutlery and china in the kitchen. Chairs scraped on the lino or banged against the piano and the echo jarred irritatingly. Father's piano, the keyboard stuffed with old documents and letters, still untouched...She imagined them, Michael talkative among his family, conferring closely around the table, exchanging news. Maureen wanted a cup of tea. And she desperately wanted to go and make it herself, the way she liked it.

She went to the mirror on the dressing-table. She peered at herself short-sightedly in the dim light, and saw a stranger there. It was nothing tangible that had changed. The features were the same. But there was a pallor and stillness in her face, a great blankness in her eyes, as if their owner had withdrawn a long way behind them. She looked too old for her short, wispy haircut, which clung limply to her temples and cheekbones.

The nightdress pulled easily over her head. She rolled it up tightly and stuffed it into the grate. Standing there on the gold pile carpet, she felt very light, almost floating, after her eight months' heaviness. She picked up the white, fringed housecoat Michael had bought her, but that, too, had a stain on it near the hem. She couldn't wear it. It would worry her. She opened the wardrobe and pushed aside the wedding dress, the fun fur, the suits and shirts, until she found what she wanted. Her father's red woollen dressing gown. It was harsh to her skin, but it was thick and warm and touched the floor all around her.

She would go down and sit there in their midst, while they were all drinking tea. They would be embarassed, afraid to look at her, not knowing what to say. Good. She was tired of ghosts.

She took several matches from the box on the mantleshelf and, kneeling, set light to the grate. A sudden warmth made her cheek tingle and illuminated the figure on the crucifix above her. The daisies darkened and dissolved in the flames and the thin cloth jerked spasmodically as the draught caught it.

Maureen watched until the last shred had furled like last year's charred leaves. Then, satisfied, she began, slowly, to go downstairs.

On Such A Bed As This

"I can see the Tower!"

"Never mind the bloody Tower. Just you get on with the bloody hoovering!"

"Come on Mum! Come on up and see!"

"Pest!" grumbled Maureen, making her way irritably up to the second floor of the guest house which she and Jason, aged eight, had taken over that morning. It was only small, but it was the best she could manage with her share of the money, after the divorce had gone through.

The guest house had five bedrooms, two of them with two double beds, two with one double and one single, and one (the honeymoon room) with one double bed. Just a nice size for one person to cope with, Maureen thought.

She found Jason in Room 5, standing on a chair on top of one of the beds, with his head poked through the skylight.

"Mum! Look! I can see the Tower!" His face shone with excitement.

"Get that chair off the bed this minute Jason," cried Maureen crossly, but she took off her high-heeled shoes (Maureen was as smartly turned out as a guardsman at all times) and climbed up to have a look. She felt quite a thrill all through her body, when she saw the top of Blackpool Tower outlined against the sky.

"Now then," she said, "no more larking about. We've got people coming in at the weekend and we've to be ready for them."

"Super int it Mum?" squeaked Jason.

Downstairs once more, Maureen set to work making sure that everything was spick and span and to her liking and Jason went off to get some fish and chips.

When he returned, the delicious aroma of vinegar and fry heralding his arrival, there was someone with him.

"It's Mr Floyd from next door, Mum," he announced, "he says would you like him to bring you a nice cup of tea?"

Maureen wasn't keen on men on the whole. She thought they were a mucky lot, not properly grown up and interested in one thing only. Mr Floyd was a stocky scrum-half-for-Cardiff sort of Welshman, with thick black hair and black eyebrows, which shot up and down involuntarily at the sight of Maureen and her superb figure.

Unlike Maureen, Mr Floyd had the highest possible opinion of the opposite sex.

"How may I be of service to you dear lady?" he cried gallantly.

"I'm quite alright thank you Mr Floyd," she replied, very cool.

"Please call me David," he said.

"Thank you Mr Floyd, it's kind of you, but we are quite able to make a nice cup of tea on our own bloody gas stove." Mentally she added, "and you can keep any thieving hands to yourself!" However she did note that although he was not wearing a jacket, he had on a dazzlingly white shirt, with a beautiful tie and even a pair of gold cuff links.

"Well," he said, "I must not let your fish and chips grow cold. Just call upon me at any time and I shall be there." Off he went through the back yard, as he had come, humming "La Donna e mobile," because naturally he had a fine tenor voice.

"Daft as a brush," said Maureen.

"She's given me three lots of chips by mistake," exclaimed Jason, delighted at the unexpected bonus.

"Then you must take them back pronto!"

"Mum!" wailed Jason. Maureen insisted on two things from her son — washing and honesty. She was not bothered how late he stayed up watching T.V., or how badly he did at school, but let him pick up a penny piece that did not belong to him, or omit to change his socks, and wrath descended on him like molten lava.

Mr Floyd popped in again several times with a piece of apple pie he had made, and then with some comics for Jason and finally to ask if Maureen could take a couple and child at the weekend as he was already fully booked.

Maureen mellowed. He was so friendly and so smart and above all, such a gentleman. Every time he came in he was humming a different operatic aria, the volume of sound increasing with each visit. She offered him a glass of sherry.

"Do you do all the cooking yourself then?" she asked.

"I do indeed. Mrs Floyd left me two years ago."

"Dead?" asked Maureen, never one to mince words.

"Oh no. Went off with one of the guests, as I was serving the soup. Leek soup it was."

"Get away!"

"I managed quite well without her. A man can do anything if he sets his mind to it." He gave her a meaningful glance from under his thick eyebrows.

The following morning, Maureen went off round the corner to the hairdresser, leaving strict instructions with Jason not to play out until the two new four foot spring interiors for Room 5 had arrived.

She had ordered them on the telephone from a wholesaler in Preston. They had seemed very reasonable in the advertisement and she did hope they wouldn't turn out to be a load of rubbish.

When she came home, hot from the hair drier, she opened the front door and gasped, then stood staring in horror at her tiny hall. It was completely filled with mattresses – four foot floral spring interiors in transparent plastic covers. There were mattresses in the dining room, mattresses in the minute private sittingroom, mattresses up the stairs and mattresses poking into the 6ft x 3ft kitchen.

"Jason!" she shrieked, "What are these buggers doing here?"

A little head with eyes like saucers appeared over the top.

"The man said you'd ordered them Mum."

Maureen began to panic. "What am I going to do? The visitors'll be coming in tomorrow. Whatever shall I do?" She seized the telephone and with trembling hands and several false diallings, finally got through.

The voice at the other end was pleasantness itself. "Oh dear...so sorry...the computer...playing up all week...they must have been intended for somewhere else...first thing in the morning...that's a promise..."

Maureen passed a sleepness night and by twelve o'clock next morning, when she had tried to get through to Preston a dozen times, she realised with dull finality that there wasn't a hope of getting the mattresses away before the arrival of the visitors. It was Good Friday and clearly the firm had closed for the weekend. She sank back against the unwanted merchandise in despair.

Suddenly through the back yard came Mr Floyd in full voice.

"Toreador on ga-ha-ha-ha-de,
Toreador! Toreador!"

Jason had not been too proud to seek help from a friendly neighbour power and Mr Floyd had responded to the call without a moment's hesitation.

Poor Maureen, her coolness gone, was actually sobbing.

"Dry your eyes, dear lady!" cried Mr Floyd, "All will be well." He scratched his head. "Let me see...we could put some in my garage...or...no...I've got it, we'll put them ALL on the beds."

"But they've got bloody mattresses on already," sobbed Maureen.

"Ah, but we shall give them *real* comfort – three mattresses to a bed. It will be wonderful!"

They toiled up and down, up and down, lifting and heaving and tugging the heavy cumbersome things, slippery in their plastic covers, until they had disposed of them all – two extra on each double bed

(the old ones on top of course, so the new ones could be returned unused.)

"Super int it Mum?" shouted Jason, leaping from one great high bed to another.

"You can get lost!" Maureen lashed out with the back of her hand, almost at the end of her tether.

"Your guests will have a marvellous night's sleep," remarked Mr Floyd, "high beds – great for making love you know. Makes all the difference!"

"Wouldn't make any difference to me," said Maureen, "I'm frigid you see, quite frigid. That's the reason we broke up. That and his smelly socks."

Mr Floyd observed the beautiful curves of Maureen's bosom, her flushed cheeks and the light brown hair curling damply on her forehead.

"Frigid?" he said, "In my opinion, that is quite impossible," and he leant across the last mattress and planted a kiss lightly on her soft mouth.

She was about to say, "Now then Mr Floyd, you can cut that out," but he was off, shouting "Back to my casserole," and breaking forte fortissimo into "Onaway Awake Beloved," from Hiawatha.

Soon the visitors began to arrive. They all seemed satisfied with their rooms and no-one remarked on the unusually high beds, except for one man who knocked on Maureen's door and asked if they could change their room as the little girl didn't like her single bed being so much lower than the double bed.
"You want to put your boot up her..." but he had retreated in horror before she finished the sentence.

It was a long day and when midnight came, Maureen was thankful to join Jason in the bedsettee in her little sittingroom. She fell at once into a heavy sleep.

Next morning at a quarter to seven, the front door bell rang. Maureen stumbled to the door, half asleep. It was a large man with a large furniture van.

"Called for t' spring interiors, luv."

"You can just bugger off again then!" exploded Maureen. "I can't get them now, they're all on the beds."

"Got to get them to Southport by nine."

"Well you can't. That's all there is to it."

"It's either now or after weekend luv."

Maureen hesitated. If she kept them over the weekend she might be charged for them.

"Can't you come back later?"

"Sorry luv."

She pondered as the cold wind blew round her bare legs. "Oh well, I suppose I'll just have to wake them up."

She went upstairs with the van man and knocked on the first door. "Excuse me, I'm ever so sorry to wake you, but the man's come for the extra mattresses...."

"What's landlady on about mother?"

"Seems she wants mattress George."

"Mattress? Not bailiffs is it?"

Confusion. People standing shivering in long-johns, glasses of water and teeth sent flying, clothes sliding off chairs, make-up swept off dressing-tables. And finally, on the top floor, a couple stark naked! But Maureen was past caring now. "Get yourselves covered up and let me get the bloody mattresses!" she hissed.

At last the bemused guests were allowed to return to bed and the mattresses were all downstairs once again. The van driver opened the front door.

"Someone's nicked me van!" he shouted, running into the street and searching wildly up and down. He disappeared round the corner and that was the last Maureen saw of him or his vehicle.

"Here we go again!" she groaned, "What a bloody nightmare!"

Serving breakfast was not easy. Carrying the plates of egg, bacon and tomato around some mattresses and over others was as perilous as an assault course. In the end, Jason stood by the diningroom door and Maureen, leaning over as far as she could reach, passed the dishes to him with demonic admonitions to be careful. Even so, one fried egg did manage to slide off the plate and into the brass coal scuttle. The little girl was in raptures and threw her egg in after it. Breakfast concluded, the father of the little girl said it wasn't quite what they were used to, paid his bill and took himself and his family to more conventional lodgings.

Later in the day, Mr Floyd helped Maureen to put all the mattresses one on top of the other in her little sittingroom. An L shaped passageway 2 ft wide was all that remained of the room. The bedsettee stood on end in the hall and the rest of the furniture went into the yard.

"Fantastic!" yelled Jason, enthusiastic to the last, "it'll be great sleeping on twelve mattresses!" They reached to within three feet of the ceiling.

Mr Floyd was even more enthusiastic than Jason. "What a truly magnificent bed," he cried, "making love on such a bed would be like floating in paradise – Solomon and Sheba!"

"I'm frigid," said Maureen, "I've told you already."

"I could cure that complaint," he said, "on such a bed as this!"

"I'm not being lumbered with all these mattresses just so you can try out your miracle cures," she replied.

Seven o'clock came at last. The ham salads and trifles had been consumed and the dishes washed. Maureen looked around for somewhere to sit in her little room. She had never felt so low in all her life. The minute the weekend was over, she would put the little guest house on the market again. She threw some sheets and pillows and a duvet on to the top of the pile of mattresses and with the help of the kitchen steps, clambered aloft. She was so tired – just a brief half hour and then she would go in search of Jason.

She awoke to find someone on the mattress beside her and it wasn't Jason. It was someone crooning "For this is my beloved, for this is my beloved," piano pianissimo.

"Mr Floyd, whatever are you up..." Her beautiful lips parted and down came Mr Floyd's mouth upon them, softer than thistledown.

"I must find out what Jason..." she murmured still heavy with sleep.

"Gone to see 'Superman' with his pal," whispered Mr Floyd, "very contented he was."

Maureen sighed, for even Solomon with all his practice, was not more adept than Mr Floyd.

David Craig

The Perfect Place

A nest, it was a nest, this hollow three or four metres broad and two metres deep, as though a giant gentle bird had cosied its breast down among the hummocks of the dunes, close-pressing but not crushing the wild thyme, tormentils, and eyebrights – its tail-feathers, white as linen, parting the blue blades of the marram grass, its broad webs and pouting crop moulding the shell-sand into this neuk as oval and rounded as an egg.

We didn't come back to the perfect place for thirty-seven years. The two-day journey from the south of England – the infrequency of ferries since the cuts – and now that we needed a vehicle, only a Land-Rover would be able to make it along that track which the Atlantic sandstorms had eaten into, tearing masses of earthy sand out of the bluff, exposing the medieval layers in the ground where buckie-shells as big as garden snails showed how this coast had thrived, before the cold wet epoch, and before the Clearances.

I helped Malcolm down from the Land-Rover, got his sticks out, his two rugs, his seven pullovers, his Thermos flask of lukewarm orange barley-water, his bag of pill bottles, his sunhat, his dark glasses and his spare dark glasses, his stool and cushions, the windbreak, the little faded knapsack stuffed with Ordnance Survey maps and ox-tongue-and-mustard sandwiches... All we needed (as I often thought at this point) was an upside-down beehive in case a wild swarm happened past.

As we inched our way along that lovely weave of purple and yellow, the little bells and stars and criss-cross texture of the machair, while my nose savoured its perfumes my mind was tensed for the first comment – nostalgic or irritable? Irritable, of course: "Have you brought the spare rubbers for my sticks? I think they are coming off. Will you look, please?"

"They're all right."

"Are you sure?" The bottom of each stick was buried centimetres deep in sand as he paused, leaning on them, a top-heavy figure beneath its load of tatty woollens, a Guy with a face as pale as a turnip, ready for the bonfire.

"Yes I'm sure. I saw when you lifted each one clear of the sand."

"Well – if you're sure – "

"Yes. I am sure."

As he lurched along the crest of the dunes a few metres ahead of me, his figure became smaller, more upright, the hair shorter, short as a boy's, his legs were bare, tanned, his feet were shod in old pumps brown with peat. "We're nearly there!" he shouted. Level with the last skerry!"

We checked our bearings, ran on for thirty yards, threw ourselves down flat in the hollow, noses amongst the thyme, hearing the bees fizzing at the trefoil flowers just inches from our ears.

"Don't move."

"I'm not moving."

"They might be pirates."

"Or a merchantman. Should I light the beacon?"

"Not till we're sure."

"Robinson Cursoe said it was the safest island."

"Crusoe," Malcolm corrcted me automatically.

"Well he did. And Man Saturday said the bad tribe never came near here, not even for wild-pig meat."

We had been embroidering our own chapters of the legend for four summers now. Each time we came to the island we were that much more independent, leaving our parents to photograph the hen harriers and ring the choughs on the other side of the headland, making the western shore into our own fastness. Malcolm raised his head cautiously, looking out to sea through the wiry lattice of the marram. "False alarm. Not a thing to be seen."

I looked. "Except those gannets."

"Rocs," he corrected me again. "Don't *spoil* it. Eggs as big as houses. They can lift up a sailor in their claws..." Then he turned and I saw a twinge of pure chagrin cross his face. "It's horrible, growing up. Suddenly I'm outside it – our game. It's just a game. Oh hell and bugger!"

Our worst word. I looked into his pale-blue eyes, under their blond-red brows, and they seemed the very colour of unhappiness. He had stopped, propped up on his sticks, and was waiting for me with an impatience that he let me see.

"Put it here," he pointed, gesturing by shoving his chin out and down. "There may be a little shelter. And we don't want to be seen."

I dropped half my load with a satisfying clatter (some day the stool might break: then what would he do?) and looked out over the sea, the beach, the machair. "Not a thing to be seen," I said. "Except those gannets."

"Fishing above the drowned village?" Malcolm was perfecting his little habitat as he spoke, rummaging the legs of the stool into the fine fabric of the flowers, placing the roll of McLeod tartan rug to prop his feet, draping the Royal Stewart over his swollen knees (those morbid totems), holding out a long, white, palely-freckled hand for each object, like a surgeon in the theatre. "So they still fish there. They can not have done in the seventeenth century, when the place was inhabited."

"The village must virtually have created a shoal," I suggested, fitting the Thermos flask into his sunhat and placing it in a rabbit-hole, where it nestled like a Surrealist photograph, 'The Lovesong of the Abortive Concept', say, or 'Convulsed in the Mirror of the Flesh'. "Like a wreck that becomes a focus for mackerel and congers."

"The village was surely evacuated?"

"Of course. I don't mean there were corpses. But sand must have built up shallowly, and the old walls turned into reefs. Perfect for flooks, and shellfish for the turbot."

"Flooks!" He made a sardonic noise through his nostrils. "They do not call them that up here – have you forgotten?"

"That's not the point…" Below his testiness, and below the pedantry of our speculations, those drowned streets were shimmering again. Our father had explained about Sulasgeir, finally abandoned in the 1650's when the sea had broken in on the common fields. After the July gales we had stared out at the line, two miles off shore, where great waves rose, whale-backed, and then, when you expected them to come combing in and in and finally burst on our beach, they suddenly reared, white chargers, shaking their drenched manes, foam spattering from their mouths. In 1956, the year of the never-ending anticyclone, we had glided out at last, in a small Cornish-blue boat with an outboard, borrowed from Crois Moraig. Dad cut the motor and we passed silently above the fathom of Nile-green, sunlit water, staring and staring (saying nothing) at the big masses down there, half shadow half object, formed into oblongs with rounded corners – the plans of houses still human, still civilised, after three hundred years of sifting and sapping.

"Well," said Dad, after we had made one more pass across the village and were headed back to the mouth of the sea-loch, "if the sea hadn't got them, the potato blight would have done it. Or the landlord's men."

"Oh *Malc*," said Mother, ruffled by this bitter taint in the sweetness of the day. "They were probably much happier in Canada or somewhere."

"Working for Reeds Paper and ruining the Indians…"

Dad's sardonic remarks had been an education: I had relished their cocking a snook at the Establishment as much as the knowledge in them. Malcolm had settled for the knowledge: information was what he had made into the caddis-case around that soft and frightened self. He was focussing his binoculars now (he carried them himself, they were his vision on black stalks) and I wondered if he could pick out that small blue image thirty-seven years away, dipping out of sight below the series of darkening crests: his illness, our parents' death in Corsica, my refusal to let him live with me.

"It's perfect, isn't it?" He still looked seawards through the prismatic glasses as he spoke. "No evidence of the twentieth century. No noise. No people."

"Quite like death."

He continued to look through his black eye-stalks. But one of his yellowish fingernails was tapping on the milled disc between the eyepieces. He shuddered as a breeze ruffled and looked sharply round as though to catch in the act this malevolent being who had it in for him, levelling chilly draughts at him from behind. I tried to turn in on myself, to revive the vision of boyhood from a little earlier, but the day was unsuitable for nostalgia. The islands were occupying the sea like hard blue bergs, stepping stones leading not to Tir nan Og but simply to the forlorn and vacant reaches of the Atlantic. I felt chilly myself, reached round for my hip-flask – but before I could ease it out of my pocket Malcolm gave me an order over his shoulder: "My lined jacket. Please."

"Your winter jacket? It's in the van. What do you think – "

"In that case it is simply out of the question to remain here."

"But – the picnic – "

"A misconception, shall we say? If only we could have made a den in the Nest..." Simultaneously we looked at the hollow, simultaneously we saw it as a shallow depression where some very small flowers just held their own against the rasping of the wind-blown sand. But I would not give in – I tried to catch his eye – he loomed away from me, looking rather like Napoleon in 1812, a few weeks after Borodinó, aggrieved at the conspiracy betwen the elements, the peasant guerrillas, sub-standard officers...I should have used the patient cunning of those peasants. But distinctly, in my head, little taut wires glowed incandescent, flamed out and burst, phut-phut-phut.

"It was your idea – that *bloody* drive, which you spun out for three days – this *bloody* God-forsaken wilderness – your suppurating clutter – " I choked on further words, words as substitutes for seizing him by the elbows, kicking away his sticks, jerking him upright and making him run run run on those sacrosanct, swaddled legs.

"Francis!" He yearned at me, imperiousness all gone, the corners of his mouth crumpling downwards like an infant's. Squeamish pity turned in my stomach. I must repress it, temper myself utterly.

"All right, then – so be it – picnic over. 'Picnic!' You're right – a period word. So let us walk straight back into the present, shall we? And if you must have this junk, you can damned well carry it yourself!"

And I set off back to the van, jogging almost, fixing my eyes on Berneray to the north, letting the mounting wind from the north-west grate my eyeballs, making them water...I should no more have looked back than Orpheus at the threshold of this world. When I did, I saw an apparition – Malcolm drawn up to his full six-foot-one, one fist clutching a stick like a sceptre, the other hand upflung at the sky, either cursing me or grasping at something, anything, as he felt his life collapse. His limbs and body were then smitten by a *rigor*, the free arm swivelled at the shoulder, palm of the hand faced the sky, arm jerked down in a straight line at the side, face (white staring face) crooked at the ground, shoulders hunched inwards. I had time to think 'The Guy on the bonfire as the flames reach him' before he crashed sideways out of sight into the hollow of the Nest.

I was sobbing as I reached him, with rage and self-disgust, not pity. He was lying on his side, a snapped stick under one leg, his head on the roll of yellow McLeod tartan, his eyes fixed open. His face looked peaceful, softened and smoothed, much younger than its fortynine years. As he felt my footsteps, he groaned, a drawn-out piteous sound that seemed to come from some other source, like a person emerging from concussion or the dentist's gas.

So I knelt down beside him, entering his aura of fusty sweat, put my right hand between his legs, gripped his right upper arm with my left hand, and rose slowly under the burden of his helpless inertia, his dangling fleece-lined boots, his middle-aged paunch (which swelled like a pudding under the inmost woollen). Pullovers fell to the ground in heaps. He lay across my shoulders like a carcass in its cheesecloth sack. The fireman's hoist, which I had learned in the Scouts thirty-six years before in the first year of Malcolm's illness. Like that I began to cart him the quarter mile that had taken us an hour and a half a little while before.

He still groaned that bewildered groan from time to time but once it formed words and I heard distinctly, "Not exactly dignified" – said almost with amusement. His beard (which smelt of rancid butter) was tickling the left side of my face and neck. I no longer had any idea what I was feeling, apart from the beard. Fine grains gave under my feet. Once when I detoured to avoid the cutting blades of the marram and followed a gulch in the sandhills, it seemed to lengthen, to turn endless on me, each step slithering backwards half as much as it had gained. Should I drop down to the firm sand of the tidal beach? But once down there would I ever get back up with this incubus weighing on me? A demeaned emotion began to curdle out of my confusion: if he was the burden, I was the beast. He should have kept hold of at least one stick to goad or thrash me with. No person should ever be so bowed under the bodily weight of another. And yet – what form of help could be more valuable, more fundamental? Advice is always impotent, lent money is a fool's paradise. In the case of my brother and me I could nearly persuade myself that I would have preferred the simple task of lifting a quadraplegic twice daily in and out of his wheelchair to the moral strain of humouring Malcolm's neurotic needs on our annual fortnight's holiday together.

Back at the road end I unloaded him into the tailgate of the Land-Rover, where he pulled himself into position on his special double seat and looked at me with something of his old overweening. I think he quite expected me to go back on foot for his life-support kit, but by now the tide was well out and I seized my chance. An old way for the Crois Moraig fishing cobles tracked through a break in the dunes not far away. I roared off through it, slurred the wheels round onto the planed sand below the belt of jetsam at the high tide mark, and drove back southwards like a madman. In the mirror I could see Malcolm jouncing helplessly like a marionette, his eyes gleaming, uncertain whether to disapprove or exult as I drove straight through shallow pools and sent water spraying and spuming all around us. And then I was bundling together the scattered pieces of his life and leaving the Nest, for good, to the mining of the rabbits and the scouring of the wind.

Mick North

P.S. Billy Pinch

I called to read your electric meter today but unfortunately you were not at home. I have left what we call a Customer's Own Reading card for you to fill in and return, the postage is pre-paid. I have also written you this letter, it's the only way I could think of for saying what I want to say, the only way to do it. People are often very nice with cups of tea and that and biscuits, even a nip at Christmas, but you couldn't sit at their kitchen tables at such times and tell them the truth of it, they'd think you were mad. It would disturb them. But someone should know.

Winter's the worst, black mornings and the cold. The week I started this December gone, it snowed, and as you'll know it didn't hardly stop until a few weeks ago. Some days the city lights were never off, or the headlamps in traffic with the snow swirling in the beams. It was like being in one of those little plastic glass efforts you shake up to make snow-storms in, it might be Bambi or something. I used to have one on my dressing-table as a boy, but not here, I'm from another place.

I hoped the snow might make the city cleaner but it didn't, only with a heavy fall at night – I'd put the first footprints up the street going to the bus-stop. The alarm goes at six-thirty, I keep it on the mantlepiece on the other side of the room. It's a bed-sit, rented, just me. I have to get out of bed to stop it. I have to be at work for eight and it takes two buses, one into town and then another out to the middle of a housing estate where the depot is. That's where you'll send the card. I need to be up early to catch the buses.

Normally I wouldn't bother so much about punctuality, but it's not like other jobs. The work's not at the actual depot, but you have to show your face and collect your book for the day, there might be Special Instructions or possibly some keys. If you're late there's nobody there – the lads are all out and it's obvious you're not, nobody there except the foreman, Smithie, and you don't know where he is. I don't know what he does once we've gone, you have to go and look for him, open-plan offices, all the secretaries look at you, the young men in shirtsleeves with ties and neat haircuts – you can't be sure what any of them do except that you couldn't do it, in your derriboots and waterproofs, you can't even get to work on time.

Smithie puts it down in a book. He'll be in a private office with one of the under-managers, and it's like you're interrupting something, the manager gives him some kind of look. Smithie gets up and walks out and you follow, back through the desks again, the men and women with nice jobs. Maybe you yourself work in an office like this, the neighbour said you both worked so you wouldn't be in. You could leave a key with her if you wanted, that'd be one procedure.

I remember my first day, I hadn't been issued with Official-Issue clothing yet, so I was wearing an ex-Canadian Air Force greatcoat on account of the snow. I sent off for it once out of the paper, it might've looked odd. Anyway, I was going round with old Ken and we had to do a little bank in the suburbs, the kind where you'd think the manager was friendly and knew a lot of his customers personally, but he asked us why were there two of us, checking our ID's, and Ken said "He's training like." The manager said "You can't imagine having to train for it, it's through here, are you both going to read it?"

It takes a week/ten days and it's the only time you work with anybody, after that you're on your own. It's not like other jobs, that's why it's better to be punctual, even a bit early, so's you can talk to the lads. But it's funny, you never really get to know anybody, and ever since I started there's a bloke called Billy Pinch has been off sick, so I've never met him. But you find yourself saying to blokes, "How's Billy, have you heard anything?" You take an interest, and some days it seems Billy's on his last legs, and then he recovers, the rumour goes round he'll be back on the job in a fortnight but then he'll have a re-lapse. I haven't asked anybody what's up.

You have to be fit in this job, all the walking, and you've got to be supple for some of the cupboards and that. I don't know how some of the older lads manage, and a lot of them ride bikes, pedals, a lot of the older ones that seem to be on the money collecting side, the slots — so it's not as if they're doing door-to-door like I do, the calls are further apart. It'd be stupid doing a whole street on a bike, on and off all the time, it'd just be a nuisance.

They look after their bikes as if they were personal property, not the Board's and they're allowed to take them home. They carry those old-fashioned sort of green oil cans with a nozzle, that just fit the little capped doofers where you put the oil in the bike, and they always make sure the tyres are hard. They've got puncture repair kits and a few tools.

I don't know how they manage, the bikes are so heavy. They've only got three gears, the old Sturmey Archers with a trigger on the handlebars, metal chainguards, "Built to last son, them, as old as you are this machine." Back home where I come from, the old man rides one to the factory, but it's only a mile or so. These lads are the same age but riding all day nearly.

Sometimes I have to take a bike, if we're in one of the outlying villages. They pile all the bikes in one van and we go in another, Wheaton, Aston, Coven, Brewood maybe, out in the sticks. I like it out there but I don't like the bikes. You don't want to be seen riding a bike like your dad's, he wears cycle-clips, and a dirty old canvas satchel thing for his baggin. It wouldn't be so bad if the bike was all right, but the ones you get to use the odd time like this are just spare, nobody maintains them. They don't even have pumps on, and there's no time to check it out before you go, so something always happens. The chain'll trip off and it's a struggle with the chainguard in the way, or I'll have a puncture.

The last time, I left it in somebody's garden, I said to the woman "Can I leave it here someone'll pick it up tomorrow." She looked at me as if I was daft. The only good bike in the depot that nobody takes out regular is Billy Pinch's, so you can't have that.

It's not as if I don't like the job. You're out in the fresh air sort-of-thing and you get to know every part of the city, it's like a special kind of knowledge. You go into all sorts of places, not just houses, places you wouldn't set foot in otherwise. I said to one of the lads, I've never been in a betting-shop before, I did Mercer's up Chapel Ash yesterday, and he laughed. He said "Billy Pinch liked a bet, sometimes he'd stake a piece of his slot money the bugger." You'd see his bike chained to the drainpipe outside and you'd know.

Then there's pokey little factories like round our way, you walk past every day without a clue but now you know – sweatshops, lines of Asian women at sewing machines, a few of the men in fancy suits in a scruffy office, smoking, gold bracelets. And where they live, the immigrant areas – doors painted turquoise, pink, sky blue, lemon yellow and that bright acidy green. Sort of icons and flock wallpaper. It's an eyeopener, you go into a room and it's full of beds.

Some of the lads despise them. Old Ken when I was training, we went into a place and he practically held his nose, made it plain like – started talking to them in his Paki accent, but they didn't bother somehow. They're timid a lot of them, maybe it's because they're illegal. Sometimes you get an old feller coming to the door in nothing but a white nightie and a stringy beard down to his knees, not a word of English but he's cackling away and smiling like he's happy, no teeth in.

All the houses you see inside, all kinds from slums to mansions just about. I like it seeing other people's houses – most of the time I do but sometimes it's terrible, doing the flats up Scotlands or round the bad estates. There was an old man who looked like a corpse, he was grey. You don't know what to do about it, you feel helpless. Then one time I had to read a meter in a pantry blocked with a bin-liner full of milk bottles, you can imagine with the stinking dregs of old milk I was nearly sick. You can't understand it, why they didn't put the bottles on the step. Other places they ask you to take your boots off, or can you come round the back. You take it all in, all that you see, until it feels like you know a lot about other people, intimate things somehow, but this is what I'm on about, it's what I'm trying to say – it's not really true is it? The lads just laugh, they say "You'll have to get a chit off Smithie for a vaccination."

You get confused. You go into maybe two or three hundred houses in a day and it's like you're not all there, I mean you're sort of invisible. I think that sometimes, when I'm walking about, what if I could just read it and disappear? Stay in a house for fifteen minutes and see what they do. I hope you don't think I'm nosey – it's just that one day you're in a nice leafy suburb, like here where you live, and you feel good. It's as if you lived there yourself. But tomorrow you're looking for a house in a street that's mostly been pulled down except for the one you're after, and the person who lives in it is just called the Occupier. The maps they give out to find your way aren't properly true, it's just an idea and people can't live in it, because when you look at a row of half-demolished houses you can see the walls on the outside that used to be inside, there's wallpaper, and those less dirty squares where pictures used to be. But it's still on the map, the sign's there, it's Brickkiln Street, you can't credit it.

Yesterday I found a dead man. He was very old – over eighty – and the neighbour said he was blind and deaf. I knew he was hard of hearing because the Special Instructions said to **Go round back and Knock Hard.** You get that – Special Instructions might say to wait a bit because the customer's lame or something. I went in because the door came open when I banged it, I had to explain to the police. His bed was in the parlour where I found him lying on the floor, you could see his shape in the bed. It was a bed somebody had been in not long before. His skin was almost transparent on the wrist where I touched him for a pulse. He was getting stiff, I could tell when I wiggled his arm a bit.

I had to tell Smithie and he put something in the book. I told all the lads because it was something to tell, they enjoyed hearing about it. Everybody tells stories, and if nothing's happened they make something up, there's a lot of gossip and slagging. A bloke'll say Ey, such-and-such got warned a while back for touching up a woman customer, or for trying to fiddle his slot returns. It's lies a lot of it, but you're never sure. Like I said, we don't see much of each other, so there's no camaraderie, what can you expect? And you yourself, you don't see us at all like, being out all day, the neighbour said. That's three times in a row now, they'll have to properly read it sometime. It's like they don't trust people – I hope you don't mind.

PS. Billy Pinch lives out Bushbury way, the new' development. I think he's married. I don't know how old he is, but if he rides a bike he must be like the other blokes. Somebody ought to know, I just picked you at random, I hope you don't mind.

PPS. Please fill in the card like I said, it'll be all right. Thank you.

Outside In

They had left her there to die, she knew.

The young one had taken away the bell so that she couldn't ring. He was clever that one; in a brutal, calculating way, but he didn't know she had watched him do it, that she always watched him in the silvery light of the room and wove what she saw into the bed-clothes with her fingers.

They'd taken her husband away too, though that she hadn't seen. They'd left a likeness in paper on the bedside-table as if that would excuse their act. It stared out at her in black and white, framed by the brown glass and efficient labels of bottles that stood like sentinels and rattled at intervals.

Earlier, the girl had drawn the curtains and switched on the light, crooning in the back of her throat as she slid her hand into the bed to feel the sheets and tipped spooned-up slops of food into the slack mouth.

After her, the man came in, whistling briskly to disguise his reluctance. She could smell the anticipation on him as he made the bottles chatter and forced the white balls down her throat. He didn't look at her, but glanced about the room as if to make sure it were empty. Then he went out and took the bell with him, holding it carefully so that it wouldn't give him away. Which was when her fingers began to dance. She had to commit the act to fibre before she forgot it.

They didn't know she could unweave blankets, or that, if she chose, she could twist from the fibres a rope and lower herself to the floor. They hadn't seen her watching spiders.

Sometimes, in the windless air of the room, the clouds in her mind would part, and she would be able to see, for a moment, beyond the walls and window, beyond the walls and door, the memory of things that were not of herself. Then she would drop the blanket and reach for the bell. Ring it so that she could tell them. . .But they were never quick enough with their muscles and strength and swiftness of foot, and when at last they stood by the bed, the clouds had already folded, and they watched her fingering her hatred into the blanket and tried to guess what it was that she wanted.

She would like to destroy them. She would like to suck out of them whatever they thought worth having. It would be her recompense, her out-of-bed settlement, her one consolation in her declining years. Or her year's declining.

But she was left with only the silence to destroy and that pressed down like another unnecessary blanket; hot and wet. Under the covers, the bed was steaming. And they, so cunning, had left her. Heartless Couple Bind and Rob Dying Woman. He had taken the bell, the young one, so she could not ring out the passage of time and distract them from their plans.

"Is she all right?"

"Yes. I've just been up. She's all right."

"What's she doing?"

"Putting on her walking boots for a ten mile hike."

"David! Don't!"

"What's the point in asking?"

"Please, just tell me"

"Nothing. Lying. What do you expect?"

"Did you check the sheets?"

"Yes."

"Well?"

"They're dry."

"Are you sure?"

"Yes."

"Did you put your hand in?"

"Of course I did."

"Right underneath? Perhaps I should check."

"For God's sake, Jenny."

"They're usually due for a change about now. I think I'll check."

"There's enough to do down here if we're going to be ready in time. For God's sake, leave her."

"It won't take a minute."

"I said Leave her."

They'd put on music. It curled up the stairs like skeins of smoke and came in under the door, bumping round the room, seeking her out.

He'd stuck his head round the door, the young one. She'd forgotten what they called him. "All right?" he'd said, and disappeared, the thief. She didn't have words now, so couldn't make him admit, when he'd clearly chosen not to, the smell of chafing sheets that made backs of legs red-raw.

Sometimes, as she lay, she would hear them shouting. His voice angry, but with half-pleading anger. Her voice softer, trying to be strong, trying not to cry. She liked to lie then, bound as she was, be-bottled as she was, and drink in what she caused. She could taste the tension in the fabric of the house and licked it up drop by drop, knowing, for a time, omnipotence.

She could hear them now below, calling to each other between rooms. What were they planning, the girl with the suppliant voice and moisture-seeking hands and the man who had stolen the bell? She coiled her hatred close and willed herself into their consciousness. They wouldn't forget. She wouldn't let them forget.

"It's almost time, Jenny."

"What?"

"I said It's nearly time. Just on eight. The'll be here soon."

"I know. I've nearly finished."

"Shall I pour you a drink?"

"What?"

"Drink?"

"If you like. Only bring it here so we don't have to shout."

"Here."

"Thank you. That's better."

"Cheers."

"David, she has got the bell, hasn't she?"

"Yes."

"You're sure she can reach it?"

"It's right next to her. She's only got to ring it."

"Will we hear it over the music?"

"Jenny, just for once drop it, can't you? Give us all a rest."

"I'm sorry. It's just —"

"There's the doorbell. Look, she's not going to come to any harm. For a few hours, just forget her."

"Sorry."

"I'm going to open the door."

The music was louder now. It was thumping against the walls and window, making them vibrate. In the bed she lay, refusing to be moved. Her fingers paddled in the water of sound and itched to ring it dry.

She had shone at parties once and sobbed in her chest to think of how she had shimmered. Men had watched her then, their eyes in search of images to carry to their beds. She had once borne laughter in her throat and her body had been real. Then. She no longer had the strength, but would like the inspiration, to make her steady way across the floor, through the door, down the stairs and into the midst of them all, charming in a floaty gown and with brilliance bursting on her lips.

The shrunken head, wispy-haired on the pillow, was adorned for a while with diamonds, with mascara and rouge, with eyes of shining energy. The words she could speak gleamed like pearls in her throat.

He'd done well, the young one, the thief, the crook. If he hadn't taken the bell, she would have rung and rung until they all came – all of them – to watch her one woman show. Standing room only, but forgive me if I remain prone. She wanted them around her bed, elbowing for a better view, so that she could lie there for their amusement and think, meantime, while they were off-guard in their strength, of some means of punishment for not inviting her to their party. And she wouldn't let the men look down the front of her gown at her body's secrets. Even if they begged on their knees.

She was the unmovable centre. The unmoving centre. And she'd prick them hard before she'd done.

"She went into decline after Jenny's father died and these past few weeks have been hell."

"But she can't be that old."

"No, she isn't."

"Must be a strain."

"Quite frankly, it's murder. She's there all the time you see. You can't get away from her."

"What about Jenny?"

"Can't leave her alone for five minutes. Always worrying, always afraid she'll come to some harm. It's an achievement to have got her downstairs tonight."

"Can't be easy for her though."

"For Jenny?"

"Watching her mother go like that."

"You're right, but I keep telling her she should try and be more detached. It's only going to mean more problems in the long run. Between you and me, it'll be best for her – for everyone – when it's all over."

Her chest was swollen with air, each breath gasped in and stored for the final expiration. In concentration, her face folded beneath the gaping blackness of her mouth, tongue flailing for the instigator.

What would it be then? What wave would she crest on?

So much for the vulgar, brassy bell. So much for its strength. It was weak – the weaker vessel. She scorned it.

There was a scratching at the door, a suspicion of suppressed human noise. Her ears cast off the glimmering, shimmering diamonds and turned back to bone to listen. What beast was at the edge of her lair? Her bubbling mouth paused on itself and turned the froth of saliva into strings to draw whoever it was into the room. Her swollen lungs freed enough air for her to suck on what could be her final act of involvement. Her fingers stopped, mid-step, their dance of invocation over the blanket ballroom floor.

The couple burst in and she could have slain them with fire from her emptied eyes. A hand, not her own, was hungry at his trouser-belt, *his* down the front of her dress, squeezing the place where her own warm mounds had once been. The couple stopped, and looked. They all three looked. There was already a lump in this bed, if an inert one. The boy and girl put their heads together and giggled. The saliva strings broke. The couple, entwined, stumbled back out.

Their exit left air-currents stirring her mind, brushing over whispers. The lullaby-voice sang of someone she had known before she ceased to be herself.

Then the air left her mind and stirred elsewhere, in her bones. The movement she no longer knew fermented in the knots of her limbs. She would untie the knots with her fingers and use the loops to snare her memories and draw them up tight to a coil she could re-live.

So then.

She stopped up her chest. Her eyes she would leave open.

They had found somewhere, warm, moving. On the bed, not in it. Arms — smooth. Fingers in hair, not blankets; fingers on skin. Lips, tongue tickling, swallowing. Hard white pellets of bitterness on her tongue. Here, swallow this. No more.

It wasn't only on the outside now. It was in. Spilling into stagnant pools in the hollows of her cheeks.

"David?"

"What is it?"

"David, I've just been up."

"Didn't I tell you not to? She's perfectly all right."

"No, no. Please come."

"Why what is it?"

"I don't know. I think something's happened."

For a while — no, less; a moment — the ceiling had moved. It became a matrix of shapes, weaving before her eyes. Its flux was the thickening of blood.

When it suddenly stopped, she thought of the bell that wasn't there to ring. And the pleasure crawled, with death, from the outside in, as her fingers fondled the glut of guilt and recrimination she would leave behind.

Tarzan's Mate

I first fell in love one Saturday afternoon at the pictures, and the man I adored was Tarzan. I was pole-axed from the moment he swung through the trees, only pausing on a sturdy branch to send forth his savage cry

I stayed for the second showing, avoiding the gimlet eye of the usherette by sinking to the floor in the darkness and squirming under seats to re-appear a few rows back. I waited through crowing cocks and bell-ringing men, urgently delivered phrases about England standing alone and shots of gun batteries silhouetted against empty skies. Waited for the moment when he would again swing through the jungle and I could gaze once more on his shining expanse of smooth chest and long shapely legs. A loincloth of respectable length always kept him decent, but in particular I remember those eyebrows, heavy and rising to a slight peak in the centre. Later he ran to fat and there was the embarrassment of stomach held in with obvious effort and teeth shining brightly white and far too orderly. But then, in the beginning, he was beautiful and powerful; totally dominant. One "Umgowa" from him would stop stampeding elephants in their tracks.

Love has a strange effect on the critical powers. I completely accepted each banal story, never wondering about that crocodile fight which surfaced in at least three films. Tarzan occupied the largest part of my thoughts, becoming the subject of frequent internal debates as to how I could supplant the simpering idiot who shared his delightful tree house.

In the small advertisements of "Picturegoer' I discovered glossy photographs for sale. Baby-sitting was not an attractive prospect but now I began to offer out my services. I made a terrible baby-sitter. One chubby soul of fourteen months brought out the demon in me. I clearly remember smacking her hands in order to behold the heart-rending sight of brown eyes filling with tears and the trembling of a sweet lower lip. To comfort her better was bliss.

Two agonising weeks passed before the postman delivered the ten by eight envelope. In familiar pose, Tarzan crouched in the fork of a tree, eyes alert, hand ready poised on the deadly knife he always carried sheathed on his hip. Gripped by addiction I yearned for more photos

The third one brought a crushing disappointment. *She* was on it too, eyes wide with fright in spite of his protective arm about her shoulders. Something more than contempt surged beneath my grey school blouse. With me by his side there would be no tackling massive crocodiles alone; I'd go with him, knife clasped between my teeth, effortlessly gliding through murky waters.

Fantasy threatened my real life. Obsessed by Weismuller, I grew increasingly more vexed with the rest of mankind. The landscape of self seemed troubled by suberranean rumblings and Tarzan made the first crack on the surface to show this disturbance.

I refused to wear my glasses, the ones with the tortoise-shell frames, for which my mother saved for six months when I cried at the prospect of wearing the cheaper steel-rimmed kind. Spectacles were hardly the thing for a jungle queen. It worried me, though. How would I swing from liana to liana when I was so short-sighted I took the stone ornamental cornucopia on the balcony fronting the town hall for a pair of cats accidentally shut out.

I quarrelled in a big way with Norma Abbott, who I'd been falling out with since we both started at St Matthew's Infants on the same day. She now linked arms witdh Pam Butterfield and even asked Miss Spencer if she could move desks. I told myself that I didn't care, although I felt in my chest a terrible hard knot that I wished would go away. So that I didn't have to walk behind Norma and Pam I went the long way taking in the southen end of the promenade.

Uncle Mick, serving in the Merchant Navy, claimed sailors never suffered eye trouble. Constant gazing out over water to a distant horizon was a guaranteed eye strengthener. I gazed and gazed until my eyes watered with the effort.

Swimming set another problem. I didn't and he'd won the Olympics with his own special crawl. From the library I borrowed 'Learn to Swim in 12 Easy Lessons', and with a pillow on the bathroom stool practised the strokes. I did this daily, performing each movement twelve times, earnestly synchronising my breath as instructed.

"What are you up to in there?" demanded my mother. I flounced around in a bad temper, shouting about lack of privacy, and stopped kissing her before leaving for school. This had been my equivalent of touching wood, and its omission left the whole day open to bad luck.

Preceding Weissmuller, God rated pretty highly with me. I won the Sunday School prize for best attender the previous year. But God languished on the starting line and now that he persistently ignored my carefully phrased entreaties was in danger of being entirely dismissed. Although I left home at the usual time, I never reached Bourne Road Chapel.

Easter came late that year. Until then the weather had been particu larly cold but overnight it turned hot and sunny enough to wear a cotton dress and plimsolls. Cousin Bernard came to stay with us. Aunt Gladys was strangely indisposed, which subsequently turned out to be Cousin Doreen getting born. Being a year younger than me until then Bernard and I had never shared any real contact.

He showed me how to lift off the fabric tape holding the base secure on the 'Overseas Mission' box, and we took out five shillings. Following his suggestion, next Sunday using money we'd snatched from starving black babies, we caught a bus out to Rippondale Woods. Apart from J Weissmuller this was the closest I'd ever been to magic.

Of course, I knew about trees. I had seen the odd specimen in neighbouring backyards but it could not compare with the sight of a whole army of them strutting in splendour across blue-bell decked grass. A huge grandfather oak dominated a clearing it had seized for itself. We stood blinking up to where its topmost branches interlaced with sky. Standing either side of it and stretching our arms we could not begin to encompass its girth.

While I was intent on proving my skill at tree living, Bernard lusted after birds' eggs. A skinny lithe boy, he determined to conquer the oak. Showing considerable ingenuity and daring, he shinned up a tree which offered footholds on the oak's periphery. Cautiously he wriggled along a branch, then transformed himself to one of the many outstretched arms of the giant. I followed his example but could not summon the nerve to make the transfer, involving a perilous forward slide on the tummy and some very nimble hand and footwork. I stayed in the lesser tree watching as he disappeared into the upper foliage but once I had my breath back, my sense of failure at not meeting the full test faded. This was me, here, up a tree! I edged nearer the trunk and stood up. Then the air was split by a treble shriek as Bernard returned. He ripped off another Tarzan-style yodel. I'd found an ally at last in an unexpected quarter. When we reached home I had splinters in my knees and Bernard's elbow bore a graze.

"How was Sunday School?" my mother enquired in a deceptively cheerful tone, which should have alerted me.

"Okay."

"And what did you do?"

"Jesus coming back and all that."

Like a cobra striking, her hand shot out and clipped me round the ear. Mrs Marshall had been round for my box and wondered why I hadn't attended for three weeks. As mother lifted the box, the bottom had fallen off.

"You'll come back here!" Mother's face boiled red with anger as she bawled after me.

Always, when Jane faced peril, Tarzan dropped from the skies to save her, but as I puffed through somebody's allotment I knew I was entirely alone. I'd never stolen before, and the enormity of my crime overwhelmed me. Not only that but I'd stolen from the needy, so God would have finished with me too. Knotted in a hanky in my cardigan pocket were coins left from the theft. I caught a bus back to Rippondale Woods.

As I approached the trees I became aware of a quality in that early evening light not present in the afternoon, almost as if someone held his breath and listened. I walked puposefully on, ignoring the blue heads I tramped underfoot. I did not pause to look at the oak, sure that if I did my courage would fail. I went straight to the tree we'd climbed before and found the first foothold.

Having nothing to lose is an asset when faced with a dangerous mission. I slid forward on the branch, taking measure of the distance between me and the oak's tantalising arm, then stretched forward, gripped firmly and kicked free, causing a frantic thrashing of leaves. I flung my legs up, wrapped them about the rough wood and pulled myself round. Elation made me feel like beating my chest and yodelling, but I needed both my arms and my breath to inch my way inwards. I didn't climb right to the top, only high enough so I could see above the rest of the trees, clear to where the town was losing itself in evening. Then I came to my senses and climbed down, confident should the opportunity arise I was ready.

During the homeward trek all thoughts of spending my life in Rippondale Woods faded along with most of the guilt about my crime.

"Umgowa," I practised in my head, and then as I came up to a farm gate, I said it quite loudly with his firm intonation.

"Umgowa! Umgowa!"

A black and white collie hurriedly drew back. With sudden warmth I remembered three aniseed balls wrapped in a scrap of paper somewhere in my satchel. I broke into a run.

Adjudicator

Hannah's father had died with a bull on top of him. A big, red, Shorthorn had crushed out his life as it knelt on his shattered rib cage and savagely raked at his face and neck with its horn. The broken body had been laid on the kitchen table by the farm hands and when the little girl had been drawn by a compulsion deep within her to view the culprit she had found it docilely chewing its cud.

As it cast a lazy eye in her direction the only visible sign of anything untoward had been some drying soil on its horn and deep plunge marks in the turf where it had thrust at and pulverised the man beneath it. It was fed and watered that evening but sometime in the night had been taken from the field and shot.

Much later in her life she married a local farmer called John Ridley. Besides being a good husband he was also an excellent stockman and always carried a stick. His idea of heaven was to prod cattle with it and he gave them the same affectionate poke whether he was buying them, selling them or just passing the time of day looking.

John kept his own bull. Entirely oblivious of the fact his wife might have thought otherwise he was taken to periodically declaring that a farm was not a farm without a bull on it. Those who might have wished to argue were met with an unmoving glare that soon persuaded them to silence.

There was no denying he knew a fine animal when he saw one. His stock bull, a placid, black and white monster called Mascot was good enough to show. Brushed until his hide shone, with his tail tuft combed into a perfect plume, Mascot won all the prizes he was asked to. He also served all the breeding cows placed before him and when these were put reliably in calf John considered his relationship with the animal to be perfect.

But Hannah thought otherwise. Bulls upset her. She hated their size, their blindness and their menace. The beast that had gored her father had been well known for its laziness. "No matter how quiet a bull is", he had once warned her, "it is most dangerous when you are least suspecting." So she could never understand how he had allowed himself to be killed.

She need not have worried about her husband. John was careful not to ignore that rule. He allowed the bull no liberties. However as time went on he did begin to worry, although his concern was different from his wife's. He thought that he might have picked a dud. Good looking and well bred as Mascot was, John was worried by his calves. They were too small and spindly. So he decided to split his eggs into two baskets and use two bulls.

Adjudicator was a huge black-sided slab of beef - even bigger than Mascot and totally unlike him. Mascot's size created the illusion of bulky comfort like that prompted by the belly of a prosperous businessman. He was solid, stoutly masculine and won prizes. Adjudicator would grace no show ring. His bulk prompted no admiration. It was the type that rang alarm bells. He was massively boned, thin waisted and fierce. He was primitive, dangerous and without subterfuge. He hated the lorry that delivered him and ripped savagely at those parts he could reach with his horns.

Hannah found her husband in the old stable leaning on his stick and looking at his latest purchase. "The herd needs a bit of bulk Hannah. This one will give it a bit more bone", he said proudly as she came in.

She raised herself on tiptoe, peered into the loose box and stared straight into the rolling bloodshot eye of the bull. From his eye she looked to his head. She had never seen one so massive. The pink lined nostrils were vibrating caverns in the wet flesh of the grey muzzle. Froth and foam hung in flecks and dibbles from his mouth. Buried in the coarse wool across his forehead was a thick, triangular steel plate which hung from two steel rings looped around his horns. A plaited saliva-soaked rope joined the plate to the thick copper ring through his nostrils. Slowly and menacingly the huge head turned. Both eyes glared at her blindly. Deliberately the bull shook his head. The rings and plate rattled threateningly. He took one slow step forward. His bulk followed. Afraid but fascinated she did not step back. He lowered his head so that she was looking down on a neck so thick that later it was to give her nightmares. Swinging his head through a narrow arc the bull crashed it against the planking she leaned against. Hastily she stepped down.

"He's too big John" she choked as she retreated from the box.

"Twenty-five hundredweight the wagon driver told me," said John reflectively. He stepped nearer the box and surveyed the bull once more. "He might be just what we need" he mused.

"Ugh!", she said, struggling to put her revulsion and fear into words, "I think he's dreadful!".

It was true Adjudicator was no looker. He was lean and dusty flanked. His dung was matted in a permanent cake to the hair on his hind legs and thighs. His hindquarters were light. So light in fact that the pendulous weight of his scrotum looked out of place. All his bulk was in his forequarters, in his head, his neck and his shoulders. He was indeed a savage looking animal.

He lay out with a batch of heifers for his first winter on the farm. The weather was hard and as the snow deepened John moved the small herd into one of his biggest and most sheltered fields. The chill of the prevailing westerlies was turned by a broad strip of Spruce and the pasture itself was broken by two open stands of ancient Scots Pine. Adjudicator was in his element. Huge, regal and proud he stalked the deepening drifts of snow, bulldozing a path for himself with his great cloven feet and low slung brisket. Surrounded by the smaller, slighter forms of his heifers he looked exactly what he was - the herd bull. When the wind rose and the tiny herd took shelter against the wood edge it was Adjudicator who stood against the driving snow with the heifers in the shelter of his lee side.

Pampered Mascot would have died if he had lain out that winter. Adjudicator thrived but destroyed his chances of keeping his freedom by almost trampling John as he shook out some extra hay.

They tried to tether him that summer but he uprooted it so easily that they tied him to a steel cable strung over an open yard instead. There he remained, huge, black and dusty, with his hindquarters more straw-matted and dung-caked than ever.

Hannah's eldest son Tom grew from a child into a lanky adolescent. He too was fascinated by the bulls and when he thought his father was not nearby he would sneak into the bull box to torment Mascot.

Growing bolder he took to taunting Adjudicator whose reaction was much more dramatic. The big bull, even more fierce in his advancing years was now tethered in a reinforced box in the old stable. Recognising his own puniness but at the same time feeling a delicious power over the captive beast, Tom would take advantage of the gangway in front of the manger. And from this position of safety would heave and jerk at the ring in the bull's tender muzzle or belabour him about the head with a stick.

The excitement, fear and dominance were too much for the adolescent boy to resist and he persisted with his torment until the bull had only to see him to roar and toss its head in impotent anger. John soon worked out what was happening and thrashed Tom after catching him but despite this the boy persisted. His father was worried and his mother was frantic.

"Get rid of it, John", she pleaded repeatedly. All her instincts required that the creature be removed.

But Adjudicator was too good a bull to cast aside. The calves he bred were too valuable and so her husband refused.

A year passed and Mascot proven in his mediocrity was sent to the slaughterhouse. His replacement caused no disruptions to the farm routine.

Adjudicator now grizzled but as raw boned as ever remained. The milk yields and durability of his daughters decreed it.

It was Market Day and Hannah left John at the cattle mart to prod prospective purchases with his stick and came back to the farm as soon as she had finished her shopping. Neat and pretty in her best suit and her feet clattering smartly in a rare pair of high heels, she came through the yard after parking her car. The stable door was shut but she could hear the bull plunging madly inside. Fearful and fascinated she turned the ringbolt and pushed open the double door. The warm stink of bull, a mixture of damp straw, rank urine, stiff dung and sweat soured her nostrils as she entered. The plank palisade of the reinforced box hid the desperation behind. Stretching on tiptoe she peered over.

Inside the animal raged against its captivity, the wooden halter block which held it banging madly against the metal stays. She was conscious only of chained strength and cruel impotence. Watching as the bull lunged suddenly upwards striving to reach something above him she saw the cause of his anger. Her son Tom lying across a rafter directly above the bull. His very presence a goad.

Fear and alarm made her knees weak. A crash and a heavy thud turned her attention once more towards the bull. He had slipped on the urine slimed cement of the stall floor. Winded by his fall he lay legs shaking and dribbling at the mouth, the mountainous barrel of his body heaving.

"Now Tom, now. Come down now" she pleaded urgently, trying to keep her voice from trembling.

"It's alright Mother, he can't get at me anyway. Look", he replied as he shimmied back along the beam and dropped into a pile of hay bales stacked in an empty stall.

He stood before her guilty and unsure.

"Why do you do it Tom?", she sobbed, brushing the hair from his brow.

The boy paused. "Because he frightens me" he muttered sullenly meeting her eyes for a moment, "and because he hates it so much."

Nodding in understanding she pushed him through the door and closed it just as the bull staggered shakily to its feet.

"You must get rid of him John" she told her husband when he came home. "He's so angry, he will kill somebody. You have got to get rid of him. Please get rid of him."

"I can't" said John stubbornly. "He's too good to go. I am putting him over Mascot's daughters. He's brought frame and milk yield into the herd. He's valuable for a couple of years yet."

"But what about Tom?" cried the mother.

John made his son promise he would not go into the stable again. It was extracted solemnly but Hannah knew he would not be able to meet it. The raging creature there had touched parts of her too. She was fascinated by his presence and despite herself she sometimes crept fearfully in to look at him. Each time she opened the door she heard the chains rattle as he shook his head warningly. Peering over the top rail she stared each time into an angry rolling eye and each time he would swing his massive skull towards her feeling for her with the top of one blunt horn.

Summer came and with it the sweet smell of fresh grass. The anger of the caged bull became worse. His bellow echoed round the empty buildings and Hannah, often alone in the house while the men were in the fields, heard him roaring and grew to hate it. The rage of the captive black monster became unbearable to her. Even John admitted he was almost too dangerous to use.

So she decided she would get rid of the bull herself. She could bear the threat of his presence and his rage at being tied up no longer. She waited until the men were working in the hay field, climbed onto a chair and looked at the guns stacked on top of the linen press. The heavy shotgun was missing. Tom had taken it hoping that the reaper would bolt some rabbits. There was a slim rifle and a puny pigeon gun. She took the rifle and climbed down. Crossing the room she opened John's desk and took a small box of shells from inside. Pausing at the back door to pull on a pair of wellingtons she tucked the rifle under her arm and determinedly crossed the yard. She opened the stable door and hitching up her skirt slipped over the rail into the gangway. Her stomach knotted with tension.

The bull glared at her over his manger. Reaching through the slats she took hold of the block and chain which held him. Drawing up the slack she strained against the beast's resistance and pulled him forward by the ring in his nose.

With awkward fingers she pulled back the rifle bolt, slotted in a thin shell and closed the chamber. Raising the gun to her shoulder she poked it between the wooden slats and rammed the top of the barrel into the coarse wool just above the iron plate in the centre of his forehead. She took a deep breath, gripped her resolve and fired. She was deafened by the crack. The great bull leaped back, his feet scrabbling wildly against the floor. He stood still for a moment and then leaped forward. His brisket smashed into the manger staving in its side and one of his horns rattled along the intervening slats like a child's stick along a corrugated iron fence.

"I can't have missed" she muttered, panic rising like vomit in her throat. She loaded again and fired.

The bull jumped backwards. This time so violently that he ripped the ring from his muzzle and snapped the half-rotten, saliva-soaked rope joining the ring to his horn plate. Unfettered, he stood for a moment, blood pouring from the wound in his nose. Then with anger bubbling deep in his gullet he launched himself at her again. The weight of his shoulders smashed the manger to the floor. His horn splintered one slat and a desperate swipe ripped out another. His hooves scrabbled wildly on the wet floor as he tried to heave himself further forward.

Sobbing in a desperate panic she loaded the feeble weapon once more. Mouthing incoherent prayers she jabbed the barrel at his forehead and pulled the trigger. The bull was undeterred. With a frenzied burst of massive strength his head was through the barrier. More wood splintered as his shoulders followed. In the few moments that he was still held fast she scrambled out of the gangway back into the stalls. Holding the rifle she ran outside, slammed the door and leaned heavily against it panting and chewing her knuckles.

She fought to collect her thoughts. There was a burst of crashing and a crackle of splintered wood from within. A series of thuds told her that he was at least free of the box and out in the alleyway.

"I must finish him off" she told herself. "I can't leave him like that". Carefully she turned the ringbolt and poked her head slowly inside. The bull as she guessed was standing sideways in the alleyway in front of the stalls.

"He can't turn it's too narrow" she reasoned. She pondered for a moment longer and then made up her mind. She slipped another shell into the gun, walked slowly up to the bull and shot him deliberately in the eye.

Adjudicator's pain filled the stable. With her ears ringing Hannah fired again into the same place. The organ was completely destroyed and hung from its socket like a monstrous burnt plum. The bull reared on his hind legs and came down with one foreleg across the top rail. All his weight followed. The rail snapped, wood and bull crashing to the ground. "He's down" she screamed, firing again. The bull thrashed on the floor struggling to rise. Even as she shot him again the beast stumbled to his feet. Adjudicator carefully arranged his legs and stood unmoving with lowered head. Very deliberately she put another shell in his eye. The response this time was a resigned shake of the head. Growing bolder she edged around and pushed the barrel against his forehead.

"Come on old man, die", she pleaded. Suddenly she reacted against his resistance. "You black devil" she screamed. And this time when she fired the bull went down on his knees as if in prayer. The massive head was lying sideways on the ground, the slender hind quarters still standing, swayed slightly, the scrotum was cruelly exposed. Twice more she fired into the back of the head, both shots hitting the area where the huge neck muscles met the base of the horn. Now there was no movement. Shaking uncontrollably in every limb she left him and went to seek her husband.

John found Adjudicator as she had left him. Shaking his head in mystification he loaded his shotgun and blasted the creature twice through the base of the skull. The body of the bull, now dead, subsided slowly to the floor.

"You can have him for nothing if you can winch him out without breaking the place any more", John told the driver of the truck from the local hunt kennels.

"No trouble" affirmed the driver gesturing to the small crane on the rear of the wagon. "This winch would pull an elephant".

Eventually the carcass lay in leaden deadness in the stable dung channel. The winch whirred again and slowly dragged the corpse through the door, up onto the tray of the truck. The purple tongue flapped from the gaping mouth. Saliva and blood still dribbled from the torn muzzle. One eye was missing. Bending over John unbolted both halves of the steel plate and slid the rings from each horn in turn leaving the massive head naked.

"Might put this on the new bull" he grunted, jangling the plate idly in his hands.

Stepping back he looked sadly at the grisly carcass of the bull that had worked for him so well. He prodded it gently with his stick.

"He was a hell of a bull that" he told the driver.

"A hell of a bull alright" agreed the man, fastening the tail board. "It will take me a day to skin him but he'll feed those hounds for a week".

Valerie Smith

The Veil

When the envelope finally arrived, the whole family went mad with delight. Hussein stood in the middle of the room, grinning foolishly, while his mother wept on his shoulder, and his sisters capered about shouting and clapping their hands. His grandmother sat on the bench, drying her eyes with the corner of her veil and saying over and over again, "Didn't I tell you? Wasn't he always the clever one of the family?" The scholarship was in his hands. The grant had been agreed. He would go to England, to study, to become an engineer. They would all be rich and he would buy a big house with piped water and their own courtyard. His little sisters would have proper dowries, and his mother would have servants to help. In the meantime he stood in the middle of the room while they fussed round him. He could hear his aunt clattering pots in the kitchen, scolding his cousins as they polished the sweatmeat trays and rummaged in boxes for starched lace cloths and embroidered mats.

In the evening he sat in the centre of the bench, his uncles on either side of him, and the villagers came in ones and twos to shake his hand and wish him well. Some of the old men, the ones who had known his father and his grandfather, stayed all evening, sitting back against the wall and exchanging solemn remarks about the dangers of foreign travel, "He's a good boy," his uncles said, "we have brought him up well. He will be safe, even in a foreign land." His mother came in and out with trays of small delicacies, the veil scarcely hiding her glow of pride in her only son. From the kitchen came the squeals of women's laughter, and the high- pitched rivery murmur of their conversation, aunts, cousins, sisters, neighbours and their cousins and sisters. Two streams of visitors, one at the house door and one at the kitchen door, came to see the boy from their village who was going to cross the sea to become an engineer.

It was a hot night, and they all slept on the roof, the tattered curtain that was supposed to seperate him from his sisters barely concealing their whisperings and soft giggles. His mother's prayers went on for a long time, and several times he caught his father's name in her special, private, yearning voice. That was her one sorrow in the day's happiness. "If only your father could have been here to see this day." At last she lay down with the little girls, and the warm dusty night settled down around him.

☆

There were so many strange things to get used to in England. Not the lessons at college - they were easy, after the strict discipline imposed by his tutors. He was shocked at times by the slovenly atmosphere of the classroom, the lackadaisical approach of his fellow-students. Did they not realise the queue waiting outside for these precious lectures? Not at all. They grumbled and chattered, arrived late, left early, skimped their homework and read magazines under the desks. Hussein found college the most restful, the most familiar part of the day.

The authorities had found him a bed-sitter, "a nice house, only a busride away," the accommodation officer assured him. It was a tall narrow house, whose every room had been converted into bed-sitters except the chilly bathroom and the clanking malodorous lavatory. All the other tenants were students, but at other colleges or on different courses. The house was noisy with radio music all day and most of the night, but Hussein's only contact with his fellow-lodgers was a misleadingly friendly "hi" as they passed on the stairs or in the hall-way. No-one greeted him when he got home, no-one saw him off in the morning. He arrived back at night tired, hungry, cold; no-one was there to take his wet jacket, to put away his books, to fetch him hot tea, to ask tenderly after his day.

He did his best to learn; he discovered various kinds of food that could be eaten straight out of a tin, he bought milk and fruit and bread, and tried to remember to eat them when they were fresh. Even in this cold country milk turned green and sour, fruit withered and rotted, bread turned blue or orange. He ate at college, or at a cheap cafe where many of the foreign students gathered, re-creating in the dingy back room the atmosphere of the village square. Here he would meet some of his countrymen, shake hands, sit for hours over the strange drink the English called coffee, and relax into the rhythms of his own language. Here they could discuss the appalling weather, the damp cold that ate into your bones, the dry cold that made your head ache, and the dismal rain that went on for days at a time. Strangeness shared became less strange.

Most of all he was astonished by the women. He had expected to be surprised, but he had not expected to remain all day and every day in this state of bewilderment. He had seen film-stars sometimes at the cinema in town, when he went to stay with his uncle. But he had thought of film stars as something special, extraordinary; he imagined them existing against a background of ordinary women, modest women, the kind of women he had grown up with. Instead, a parade of film stars confronted him all day long. Young, old, married, single - even pregnant wives and innocent virgins marched past him, stared him in the eye, flaunting half-naked bodies until he did not know where to look. Their legs were bare to the knee, sometimes almost to the secret places; their dresses short and tight, their breasts exaggerated by underwear that was on open display in public shop-windows. Most of all he was distressed by the unashamed boldness of their impression. They did not lower their eyes as they passed, but fixed him with a direct, candid look. Some of them even smiled at him, an inviting smile, a smile that he thought existed only on the bad girls of the city. And these were not bad city girls, but students, the daughters of doctors or teachers; even the teachers themselves used the same bold gaze, standing so close to him that he could smell womanly skin and hair. He kept his own eyes cast down in a state of perpetual confusion.

One day he was sitting in the bus on his way back to his bedsitter from an evening class. There were very few passengers at this dead time of the day - most people were at home eating their supper or watching the television, and those who were out were sitting comfortably in pubs or cinemas. The bus stopped to pick up a solitary passenger, and a middle-aged woman got on, laden with shopping bags, trying to balance them all in one hand while she fumbled for change in her purse. The bus started with a jerk, she stumbled against Hussein with all her shopping, and he put out his hand to steady her. She looked at him to thank him, then looked quickly away, stepping beyond the reach of his hand. She wore a thin brown coat, longer than usual, the skirts flapping well below her knees, a coat buttoned all the way down the front, neatly belted at the waist; all her hair was tucked under a big headscarf with a faded pattern of green and brown flowers. She sat on the other side of the bus, her shopping piled in her lap, and her tired round-shouldered slump reminded him of his mother at the end of a market-day.

Two stops before his own, she picked up all her bags and made her way down the bus, her face turned away from his as she passed. The headscarf was pulled tightly down over her forehead and knotted under her chin as close as a veil. Only her pale, unlipsticked mouth and her downcast eyes could be seen as she stood by the driver, waiting for her stop.

"This ain't Bromley Crescent, mate," said the driver.

"It doesn't matter," said Hussein, getting off the bus behind the woman and waiting to see which way she would turn. She paused for a moment, put down her bags and flexed her fingers, then picked them up and set off along a quiet side road. She did not stride wide-legged, straight-backed, down the middle of the pavement, like other women; she went slowly along in the shadow of the hedges and walls, balancing her shopping, stooping over its weight. At home, women carried loads five times as heavy as this for miles, but he had learnt different ideas in his months at college. He would help this poor woman: he would lighten her load, he would act like a polite Englishman, and at the same time pay a tribute to his own concept of women's proper nature. She would be pleased and grateful; she would invite him in, and give him the best chair, and offer him tea in china cups, and home-baked cakes.

He hastened his stride and she glanced at him nervously over her shoulder, quickening her pace. He marched up behind her until he was just level with her, and he could hear her rapid breathing as she hurried along. He fell into step beside her, unable to see the expression on her face for the concealing scarf.

"Can I help you?" he said politely, in his best accent.

"No, thank you, no thank you," she replied in a hasty mutter.

"Oh, but please. Those bags...they are so heavy...a woman of your age...you should not be carrying such heavy loads ...you should not be alone...is there no-one to look after you?..."

He put out his hand to take the shopping bags from her, and she pulled them away, staggering back into the hedge and shouting, "not my handbag, leave me alone, leave me alone..." He put out both hands to help her, to stop her falling into the scratchy privet, and she swung the bags at him so that he lost his balance and fell heavily on top of her. She screamed as his weight descended upon her, and spat in his face as they slid to the gritty pavement in a confusion of twigs and leaves and scattered shopping. He tried to help her up, but she fought and struggled as he held her arms, and her scarf fell backwards, freeing her thin grey hair.

Lights flashed on in the neighbouring houses, and hands grabbed at him from behind. The woman was sobbing in someone's arms, and the man who had held him was shouting a stream of filthy names in his ears and kicking him on the ankles to make him walk.

In the police-station he wept and tore at his hair, calling on his mother's name to swear his innocence. It had no effect at all, in fact it seemed to make the policeman more angry than ever, and when Hussein realised this he calmed down and tried to make his English perfectly comprehensible. A college student, he felt insulted by their offer of an interpreter. He would provide them with all the proper answers for their official forms. He was locked in a cell, on his own; from their rough remarks he gathered that this was an act of kindness, of protection. There was a narrow wooden bed, a coarse blanket, a stone wall by his head, stuffy smells of stale smoke and heat and ancient urine, noise all night of other people talking, shouts and a quarrel in the small hours of the night. He fell into a dream of sleeping at his uncle's where it was all just like this and yet utterly different. In the morning, instead of the smell of fresh woodsmoke and peppermint, there was a thick white mug of tea, sweet, milky and stewed, and a reek of disinfectant.

The interview went on for days. Interviews at the police-station, interviews with a social worker and a psychiatrist, interviews at college with his teachers and the principal and the welfare officer. The welfare officer sent him to a Citizens' Advice Bureau, and they sent him to a lawyer, and there seemed to be hundreds of forms to fill in, letters to understand and to answer. He could not comprehend that they wanted him, an innocent man who had only tried to be helpful, to plead guilty to a wicked crime.

"You don't want to put that poor lady through the ordeal of the witness-box, now, do you, lad?" said the policeman.

"It won't look so good in court, you know," said the lawyer, shuffling her papers and looking embarrassed. "It's your word against hers, and she had a lot of bruises."

"I didn't mean to hurt her, I was trying to help," said Hussein, trying not to weep, for it annoyed his lawyer nearly as much as it annoyed the policeman. "I was trying to help her up and she struggled. You should see the bruises on my leg where that man kicked me."

The trial itself passed in a confusion and a blur. Hussein was pushed here and pulled there, told to speak, told to be silent, asked questions by one person and ordered to give the answers to another. The woman sat in the witness-box, trembling, and her voice could hardly be heard. She had pulled her scarf down over her forehead, her cheeks were hidden, she turned her eyes away from his pleading gaze. In the end, his exemplary college record and the testimonials of his teachers saved him: he was found guilty, but put on probation. They all seemed to think that he should be grateful: teachers, lawyer, social worker, they all came up to him afterwards, expecting congratulations.

All he could think of was his mother's expression, when she received the letter. It was not the worst: he could stay in this country, he would finish his studies. But the embassy kept an eye on its students, there would be a mark against his name in some list. His mother would read the letter. She would pull down her veil to hide her gaze, and stoop a little more, as though carrying a heavy burden.

Mud Bastard

Kevin watched the three boys as they filed into the gulley that led down to the culverts. That was where the river came through the railway embankment. Today they had no gun. Once he had seen them shoot a robin with their air rifle. Red blood on the red breast; he had never forgotten it. They called him Mud Bastard. He'd never found out why. He supposed it was because he was fat, or because he had no parents: because they hated him. He was lying on the tarpaulin roof of his grandad's pigeon cote. Beneath him he could almost feel the sobbing cries as they bubbled in the birds' throats. The roof was black and hot. Kevin half-turned to scratch his leg. In the intense light it looked as white as suet. He settled back, waiting for the boys to appear again. All around the river grew thickets of willow-herb. From where he lay it looked like clumsy purple brush-strokes on a child's painting. It was sending out a fine mist of cotton-like spores which drifted up into the gardens, setting seed in the more neglected ones. His grandad hated the stuff: 'Fireweed' he called it. Kevin dug a filthy fingernail into a bubble of tar on the roof. He caught the faint shouts of the boys as they emerged from the far end of the gully and gathered on the little bridge that went over the river. It was so hot that the top branches of the big sycamore tree shimmered in the air. He'd peered through a piece of ice once and things had looked like that then, but cold. He turned over on his back. Behind him lay fields, the river, railway, canal, farms with cows in their fields. This side, rows of houses followed the old river terraces and the hulks of mills rose above their dark slate roofs. Through a gap in the houses he could watch a constant stream of traffic which rumbled in and out of the town.

Kevin lived in the end house with his grandparents. His parents were dead, or somewhere else, or he had never had a father. No one had told him, except in the insults they threw. The Mud Bastard. His grandad worked the nightshift at the mill, his grandma did days at the Co-op vinegar works. She always smelt of stale vinegar, as if she was being slowly pickled. Today was a Friday in the school holidays: his grandad's night off, so he was in the pub with a pint in his fist, playing darts, or maybe bowls, since it was a fine day. Soon he'd be home to have lunch - a bacon muffin or a slice of pie with some of the pickle his wife brought home. Kevin turned back to watch the boys who were gathered aimlessly, looking down at the water. Once they'd tipped some barrels from the dye works into the water and it had turned dark red, like a biblical river running with blood. The roof sloped back towards the house, so he could watch without being seen, peering over the edge. The Mud Bastard is watching, waiting. He knows everything you do. Waiting. Waiting for his grandad. Waiting for the boys to leave his territory. Kevin slid carefully off the roof and brushed at his filthy shirt front . He'd catch it off his grandma. He took the peg out of the fastener and carefully prised open the stiff door of the cote. Quickly, he slid inside. There were six birds, white ones and soft grey ones. Racing pigeons. Sometimes Kevin went with his grandad to let them off. Somehow they found their way back through miles and miles of air, always knowing where they were going, always sure in the emptiness. They clucked in alarm at Kevin's approach, jerking backwards on the perches. Their eyes were expressionless, the yellow irises like coloured glass. Kevin dug his hand into a sack of corn that stood by the door and poured a golden trail into the feeding tray. It was like the nuggets that men had killed each other for in the Klondike. He held a single piece out towards the birds, but they shrank back from his hand. They would never come to him as they did his grandad. He stood watching them, the faint sounds of the world outside filtered by the stillness of the cote. Finally bored, he went out again into the blinding sun, fastening the door behind him and shading his eyes to look down the long dirt back. It was as if the sun had drunk all colour, bleaching the walls of the houses.

Kevin's grandad was making his way unsteadily along the back where the neighbours threw their ashes. A group of small children who were playing with a skipping rope made way for him fearfully. He was in his shirtsleeves, holdilng a paper bag of muffins in one hand. With the other he touched the wall beside him, looking straight ahead, like a blind man. Kevin saw him wipe the sweat from his forehead, ruffling his wild grey hair, then tearing at the collar that constrained his fleshy neck. As he approached the boy dodged behind the hut, unsure, watching.

"Kevin!"

It was more like the call of a crow or a magpie than a human voice, harsh and ragged. He didn't answer and the voice came again, muffled this time.

"Kevin!"

When Kevin turned to look his grandad was pissing unsteadily against the midden door, where they threw their rubbish and the dustmen came with shovels. He was in full view of the neighbours. A fine spray was rebounding down the front of his trousers, glistening in the sun like dewdrops. He kept throwing out his free hand behind him in little balancing movements.

"Kevin!"

"What?"

"Whar? Come for your bloody dinner, that's whar!"

Kevin came round the end of the shed as his grandad was trying to mount the steps into the back yard. He stumbled, dropped the bag, then stooped forwards to grope for it, falling onto his hands and knees and going up the steep yard almost in one lunge, like a bear. Coming behind him into the house Kevin heard the far-off cries of the boys. He turned to see them flicking some dark object high into the air, gathering around as it fell, a distant black dot. They had found something; something soft and alive.

In the kitchen Kevin's grandad was hunched over the stone sink with his braces hanging down from his waist. He was retching intermittently, his eyes glassy, like those of the pigeons. Suddenly, a great belch of brown vomit gushed out and the hot kitchen was full of the stench of stale beer and sick. The big man spat then straightened up, wiping his mouth with the back of a hand, shuddering. His small blue eyes had rolled upwards, showing little cuticles of white beneaath the irises. It was like the face of a dead man. The boy was afraid. He kept close to the open doorway. There was a streak of vomit across the flagstones of the floor and down the front of his grandad's shirt; a dark, damp patch had formed on his grey trousers from clumsily relieving himself. He took a step towards Kevin who stood in the doorway, then steadied himself, both hands grasping the back of a chair. The knuckles were white and he grinned in a ghastly, forced way, sweat glazing his face. It was like the way he smiled when the Welfare woman came.

"Dinner! S'ave sum dinner."

He swayed, steadying himself against the chair, resisting the terrific pull of gravity that wanted to drag him down. The bag of muffins lay crushed on the table.

"I don't want any."

The blue eyes blinked in disbelief. He cocked his ear as if he was listening to the wireless, to some faint crackly broadcast from a far country.

"Wha?"

"I'm not hungry."

The big man took a hand from the chair back to wipe his face and almost fell.

"Nor hungry? Wha the bloody 'ell, d'ye mean? I've got summat."

"I don't want owt."

The glassy eyes blinked furiously.

"Don't want owt is it? Yer kekky little bastard!"

The man lunged forward aiming a blow at Kevin's head. Kevin ducked, but his grandad fell against him, toppling them both out of the doorway and over the step into the yard. Kevin heard the crack of a head as it struck the yardstones. He rolled free of the bulk of the man and crouched in the corner. His grandad lay on the yard with one leg still inside the house. A thin trickle of blood rolled down from a graze on his temple. The blood was very dark against skin that was as white as fungus and sweating a thin mucous. The man raised his head, eyes unfocussed, and started to vomit quietly onto the yardstones. Slowly, semi-conscious, he ceased, his head subsiding into the congealing pool. Then he went to sleep, snoring almost at once in raw, shallow breaths.

Kevin didn't dare move. He stared at the fallen man from a corner of the yard. Had anyone heard? Would a crowd of people come rushing to offer help? He dreaded the thought, cringing inwardly at the shame of it. No one came. After a time he stood up unsteadily. He took a step towards his grandad and bent down to listen. The man's breathing came in steady rasps, like a piece of iron being slowly filed. He was dead drunk. Kevin touched his shoulder.

"Grandad!"

There was no response. The man had entered oblivion. He tried again, this time shoving at the shoulder so that the body rocked from side to side.

"Grandad! Wake up!"

Still nothing. The boy put his hands under his grandad's armpits and tried to drag him forward, so that at least his feet would come out of the doorway, but his own feet skidded in the pool of vomit and he lost his grip. He was unable to budge a weight that was heavy with futility; its sheer lack of life defeated him. He smelt his grandad's strong sweat on his hands and wiped them on his trousers.

Kevin went down into the garden and unfastened the door of the pigeon cote. The dim light and the soft, soft, cooing of the birds was like a sanctuary. The thought of the man lying up there in the back yard made him feel sick, the kind of nausea that comes from a blow to the head. Kevin had banged his hip against the wall as he fell. He pulled up his shorts to look at the faint bruise that was forming. It was the same colour as the blue in the plumage of the birds. His grandad's birds; they wanted nothing to do with him. He waited, imagining his grandad's voice at any moment, but there was nothing. After a while he left the cote, and went into the garden. The boys had gone from the stream and there were no shouting voices. Kevin went slowly with his sore hip, down through the garden, past the neat rows of his grandad's cabbages, past the big rhubarb patch. Two white butterflies went by, interlocked in a wild dance, their wings trembling through the air. There was a paling missing from the garden fence and he was easily able to squeeze through into the meadow beyond. For a time he sat in the thicket of ferns that grew at the edge of the field, breathing in their strange, minty scent. He watched the gully and waited. There was no one. When he was certain of this, he stood up and went foward through the waist high grass, its seeds sticking to his sweaty legs.

Kevin ducked into the gully, afraid of an ambush, and almost ran to the river. A magpie flew past him out of the scrubby elders, startling him for a second. His heart beat hard upon his tight chest. For a while he stood on the bridge looking down into the filthy water. Everything seemed still and peaceful. Then he saw the frog laid out across an old car tyre in the full heat of the sun. The boys had thrown it up into the air and let it fall on the hard path, catching it by the leg and flicking it up, again and again. Kevin had watched the game before, he knew that look on the boys' faces, half horrified, half hysterical with laughter as they felt the living thing give and twitch under them. Afterwards, they had pinned it down like a crucifixion with a stone on each foot, so that it lay on its back under the terrible sun. Kevin knelt. He was close to the black mouths of the culverts. One by one he took the stones from the frog's feet. Its skin was baggy and loose. All over its body there were grazes. Dust and tiny stones had been driven into the thin skin. The frog twitched feebly as he touched it and he drew his hand back, suddenly appalled. He watched it struggle with its broken back. Its long back legs stretched out uselessly. They looked like the pale legs of a girl. He turned and broke off two stems of Himalayan balsam from behind him. Their foetid smell made him want to retch. Carefully he manoeuvred the frog onto them, as onto a stretcher, and carried it down to a little sandbank that made an eddy in the river. Here he floated the frog out on the stems and watched it carried slowly away, jerking its front half feebly as its body tried to re-connect a broken spine.

A flight of six pigeons went overhead. They flew in a smooth circle above the houses, wheeling like handfuls of torn paper. They flew over the man who lay unconscious in the hot yard, the only things he had loved. Kevin watched them. He felt uneasy. Had he fastened the door of the cote? Did it matter, because they would return wouldn't they? But for him? Would they come back for him? The thought was like a hot needle, jabbing, jabbing at his brain. Had he...but the voices broke out in front of him:

"Mud Bastard! Mud Bastard!"

And the boys emerged one by one from the tunnel, their chanting faces as stiff as masks, stepping from darkness into the blade-hard light.

The Oakum Room

We recognised the quick step and the slap, slap of Mrs Hanson's shoes as she walked along the corridor towards us. The sound stopped outside the door of the oakum room, where we worked. She came in and walked to the raised dais in front, fanning the air, thick with the oakum dust, away from her face.

"Put down your work."

I glanced across at Polly. We were never told to stop our work. Not before it was time to go down the corridor to the dinner hall, where we sat in straight rows facing the front, to eat our potatoes, and the thin liquor that they called gravy.

"All those between the ages of sixteen and thirty rise."

Again I looked a question to Polly, but we both rose to our feet. Mrs Hanson was not one to cross if it could be helped. I rubbed my raw hands together, trying to remove the sharp particles of rope.

"One of you young women is to be most fortunate. There's a Mr Jarrotson, a decent farming man, has asked permission to choose himself a wife. He needs a clean, strong woman and of course she must be of childbearing age."

A murmur of suppressed excitement flew around the room.

"He's here now, and wishing to make his choice. You're to go to the female ward, wash yourselves and make yourselves as decent as you may. Then you must attend the main waiting room, where I will meet you, and escort you inside. You will be presented to Mr Jarrotson. You are most fortunate to be given this chance. Go now."

There were twelve of us all pushing past the older women to get to the door. I saw Clara Flint picking nervously at her worn gingham smock...the workhouse uniform.

"Not you Flint," Mrs Hanson's voice snapped out.

Clara turned away, the distress showing in her huge eyes, with the violet shadows beneath. She returned to her seat, shoulders shaking with the coughing that she tried to suppress.

"And not you Clark."

Annie Clark turned round angrily back to her work. Annie was at least forty, but she was tough and bossy. I didn't know how she did it, but Annie didn't seem as 'got down' as the rest of us.

Old Nelly Parker grabbed my sleeve as I passed her.

"Smile tha best Susan, and tha'll not see me again."

We hurried down the corridor to the female ward. It wasn't the usual slow shuffle that moved us round our workhouse world. Special extra jugs for washing had to be fetched and a great palaver followed, with fights and hair-pulling, over Margery's comb. There was a great pinching of cheeks and smoothing down of shabby clothes.

"Tell me how smart I look Susan," said Polly. "Have I got my apron straight. I wish I'd done a bit of goose grease for my hands."

"You look fine," I told her. "I hope you get picked, though I'd miss you sore. There's nowt that any of us can do about our hands".

I tucked mine beneath my apron, red and raw from the hours of unravelling rope, that we called oakum picking. Soon they'd grow hard and calloused, like the older women's hands. Scarred and tough like the skin of a beast.

"Now you think of the bairn Polly. Maybe he'd take the little one too, if you be chosen. You could be together Polly, you and your little son...not catching a glimpse of him now and then, when they've the charity to let you visit."

We'd both arrived at the workhouse on the same night, me and Polly. I can't think how we'd have managed if we hadn't had each other.

Mary pulled Janet's hair down, and she screamed and hit back. Janet's wirey hair was hard to keep neat. Eliza Beck snatched little Nancy's clean apron, and shoved her grubby one in its place. Polly pulled Nancy's clawing hand away from Eliza's cheek.

"Nay love...tha's prettier by far than Eliza. Tha'll look best whatever."

We hurried back down the corridor, and across the open yard to the main building, where Farmer Jarrotson waited. All pinching and pushing at each other to try to be first. The great entrance loomed above us, and we slowed our steps. There was the high porch and columns...the ornate clock and flight of steps.

I stopped and took Polly's arm. A flood of despair washed over me. I'd stood looking up at those columns that night that I'd carried our Peter in my arms. That night that I'd guessed he was dying, and I'd thrown away my last scrap of pride.

We'd managed well enough after Mam had died, until Peter fell sick, then I couldn't work for he needed me. In the end I'd no money for medicine, no money even for food. I brought him to this dreadful place, hoping to save his life, but he'd died that same night, and still I couldn't forgive myself for not bringing him sooner.

I clung to Polly, she was the only warm and lovely thing I'd found since that miserable night, and Polly had more reason than me to get out.

"I'm thinking of our Peter," I said.

"Aye…I know you are, and I'm thinking of how you sat with me that night, and helped me nurse my little lad, though they'd taken your brother away."

Little Nancy took my other hand, twisting the end of my sleeve. I put my arm around her then, remembering how she stole scraps of cloth from the sewing room, to make dolls for Polly's child. Eliza stopped in front of us, she turned round and looked at Nancy. She undid the apron and handed it back.

Nay…you have it," said Nancy. "I don't know as I want to get chosen."

Those two would sit together in the evenings, singing songs and whispering about the happy times they'd once had. We seemed to huddle closer together. No one wanted to start to climb the steps, but the door opened and Mrs Hanson came out.

"No need to wait around. Come here. Go into the waiting room. Make an orderly line."

We followed meek and silent. Polly and I were last. We waited…heads bowed, faces to the floor, hands beneath our aprons.

"Now Mr Jarrotson, come and make your choice. I'll say the names. This is Foster. Small of stature, but clean and strong. Childhood rickets I dare say. This is Pearson…a decent enough girl, though her mother's in the asylum ward and her father is often in the vagrants' side."

I looked up and saw that Farmer Jarrotson was a fat man of about fifty, with greying sandy hair. His clothes were new and made from good cloth. His small grey eyes darted from face to downcast face, his cheeks flushed with enjoyment at the task.

I think it was Eliza who started it. As Farmer Jarrotson passed her, he lowered his eyes to her long thin legs, and something of a sneer touched his mouth. Eliza suddenly crossed her eyes. Jarrotson moved quickly on to the next woman.

As he moved down the line, women developed coughing, shaking, violent itching and dribbling at the mouth. The man moved faster down the line, Mrs Hanson following, furious in his wake. He reached the end of the row where Polly and I stood. I echoed Eliza's crossed eyes and brought my swollen hands out from beneath my apron. He turned from me to Polly.

Polly was still, staring at the floor. Her soft brown hair combed smoothly to the side.

"Ah," said Mrs Hanson. "Polly Allsop. She has a young child over in the infants' ward. Father unknown, of course…still, proof of childbearing."

Jarrotson smiled his relief. His hand went out to grip Polly's shoulder. Polly looked up into his face. A quiver ran through her body, then suddenly, mouth snarling, teeth bared, she lunged at his hand, biting hard and catching a pinch of flesh. He pulled back, his face gone white with shock, and went towards the door. Mrs Hanson's hand shot out, slapping Polly hard across the face, knocking her to the floor.

Eliza's big mouth cracked open in wild laughter. Then the fancy-decorated, high ceiling of the waiting room, echoed with wild gushing laughter, as we all joined in.

Jarrotson's eyes flashed wide with fear.

"I'll have non o' them."

Mrs Hanson opened the door and ushered him out, though we could see that he couldn't wait to be on the other side.

Our laughter subsided as Mrs Hanson returned, her face red with anger.

"Leave her be," she shouted at me, as I'd bent to help Polly to her feet. "You wicked women. You disgrace your charitable benefactors. You will know the wrath of God before tonight. Since you cannot bear to leave your oakum picking, you may keep at it all through the night. There'll be no more chances...I'll see to that."

The main door opened and the woman known as Jeevers came in, followed by one of her tall, thick-set helpers. We recognised well enough the shape of the strait-jacket in her hands.

Hanson pointed, and they went to pick up the unresisting Polly.

"File out," bellowed Mrs Hanson.

Slow and quiet we moved towards the door. Heads down, shuffling feet. Back across the cold yard...down the stark tiled corridor, back to the oakum room.

Neil Roberts

The Wedding March

A crowd of wedding guests, balancing drinks and informally arranged in order of importance, blocked the pavement outside the hotel entrance and spilled into the road. Nearly in the middle of the road, a kneeling photographer was taking his final shot as the dark blue Cortina rolled away, shaking off confetti. The groom's attention was already fixed on the junction ahead, but the bride was making her last offering to family and friends, and taking a last impression: of the threads of her life gathered, for the only time ever, in a colourful pattern that signified herself, and behind them the building like a wedding cake, functionless columns and Snocem walls on which were sprayed, in fresh red paint, the letters NF and above, in the same colour but a different hand, SMASH.

Then the car had turned into a flow of traffic out of town. With her arm on the back of her seat, where she had rested it to wave to the guests, she looked at the young man's profile.

"Husband," she said.

"Not hubby?"

"No. Husband is quite sexy somehow. I never thought of it before."

"Wife isn't."

"Oh, aren't I?"

"Yes," he said, and looked at her, deliberately, as if seeing her for the first time, in a way he knew excited her.

They were on a cantilevered dual carriageway, passing a vast Double Rank fun palace which loomed from below the level of the road. The traffic was surprisingly sluggish, and the car muttered along in second, to the rhythm of the blinking brake lights ahead.

The bride was nineteen years old. Her face was small and regularly featured, pretty like an everlasting flower, as if some vivifying and corrupting substance had been omitted from its composition. Her husband, who was a few years older, had several of the properties of a statue, in particular there was nothing in his appearance that looked accidental, but unlike a marble statue he absorbed a great deal of light. His thick black hair rested in a cultured curve at the bottom of his collar. He was thawing from an attitude of tolerant boredom into contemplation of an enticing future in which his bride represented the element of ecstasy. He was a young man with prospects.

"Tell me about your stag night," she said.

"There's not much to say about it. A lot of people got drunk."

"Not you, of course." She adopted an ironic tone but only as a formality: she saw in the contemptuous stretching of his lips that he had not got drunk. She could so easily imagine him sitting among his friends, all of them more or less pissed, his mouth tightening now and then in just that way, but mostly amused: contemptuous, tolerant, utterly apart from the welter of male immaturity. It was, in fact, the mental picture that represented her love for him, and she accepted his familiar aloofness from the sentiments of the wedding day.

"That's real life to them," he said. "It's what they look forward to and remember and talk about. They're all no-hopers really, all but one or two."

They were driving to a seaside town, to a hotel and a bed in which would begin an embrace uninterrupted, then and forever, by the exigencies of courtship and parental roofs. That bed was the entrance to a life, enclosed by a crystal sphere of radiant and dependable love, within which was a time-machine of children, orgasms and worldly success (a little differently disposed in the perspective of each) and outside which the world might arrange itself as it pleased.

If the car were travelling smoothly onward, it would be a gratifying model of that sphere, but the traffic had now stopped altogether, and it was like a blockage in their bloodstreams. The young man banged his fists on the steering wheel. His wife leaned her head on his arm and said,

"Let's talk about what we'll do tomorrow, and the day after, and the day after that, for ever and ever, and we won't notice the hold-up."

"I want to be doing it, not talking about it," he said, holding on to the steering wheel with rigid arms.

"Oh, talking about it, looking forward to it, is part of doing it, it's half the fun. We'll make love three times before breakfast, then we'll make love again instead of having breakfast, then we'll lie on the beach for two hours and have each other for lunch..."

The kiss that she won from him was interrupted by the broad shadow of a policeman falling through the driver's window.

"I'm sorry about the hold-up sir," he said when the young man had wound the window down. "We've had to cordon off Urmsley Road because of the demonstration."

The driver looked up into the policeman's massive, bearded face. "What demonstration?"

The policeman leaned a little closer and his helmet knocked gently against the edge of the roof. "The National Front," he said with studied impersonality.

"Isn't there an alternative route to the motorway?"

"There is but it's jammed already. You'd be better waiting while the main road clears." He walked sedately to the car behind.

"Fuck politics," the young man said. "People with big ideas blocking the public road. They talk about freedom but they don't give a damn about ordinary people. They're all the same."

The traffic had finally stopped in an area to the east of the city, between the centre and the main industrial estates, once a large working-class suburb of late Victorian terraces. Now most of the houses were empty, the shapes of their windows recalled by grey breezeblock squares. Interspersed among these shells were incongruous facades of bright paintwork and neat curtains, as if got up for a period film.

"I used to live here," the bride said suddenly.

"What?"

"Until I was five. Before we were rehoused. There!" She pointed to a street leading off the main road a few yards ahead, where a stationary line of cars curved off in a thwarted detour, like a junction in a railway track. Beyond a jagged end of brick an empty space yawned. Though it was hidden from the angle at which she looked, her mind's eye clearly saw the bedroom fireplace hanging in mid-air from the adjoining building.

"Why should they want to hold a demonstration here?" she said. "Nobody lives here."

"Nobody? Only about five thousand Pakistanis." He pointed across the road to the city's only surviving suburban cinema, on whose wall a beautiful young Asian couple stared chastely into each other's eyes, among the incomprehensible punctuation-marks of Urdu.

Through the lowered window of the car a sound was gradually amplified. At first it was an undifferentiated roar, like a building collapsing over and over again, then a repeated rhythmic cluster played on a deep, resonant wind instrument: a monotonous three notes with heavy stresses on the first and third. The young man in the car found himself banging the heels of his hands on the steering wheel, to the rhythm of the noise.

"What's that sound?" the girl asked after he had been doing this for some minutes.

"People chanting."

"There must be thousands of them. Where are they?"

"Up ahead somewhere. You heard what he said."

"What are they saying?"

"You've got ears as well as me. Probably Piss Off Shit or something equally intelligent."

"Are you sure it's up ahead? It seems to be all round. I think it's frightening."

"Being in a car distorts your hearing. And since we *are* in a car, we're safer than at a football match. Anyway there's dozens of police."

As he spoke the policeman who had apologised for the demonstration ran past, along the middle of the road, holding something long in his right hand, his heavy coat thumping the air as he ran. The girl in the car caught one profile flash of his face, which wore an expression of such unbelievably distorting ferocity that her recognition did not catch up with him till he was well out of sight. His running bulk in its heavy coat, fuelled by that terrifying rage, might now be crashing through cars and buildings.

"Love, I *am* frightened."

He wound up the window and held her wrist in his hand. The unscratched gold of his wedding ring bit comfortingly into the bone of her wrist. "Just don't get hysterical," he said.

As if a vast, thick steel door had been opened the noise was suddenly everywhere, the car was vibrating with it, and at the same moment hundreds of people gushed out of the demolished street on their left. The people at the head of the crowd looked about them as they entered the main road, momentarily resembling hikers consulting directions then, as the crowd welled behind them, merged into a convex meniscus around the neck of the side-road, engulfing the cars that had turned off.

The girl in the car briefly saw, through the window of a house, the face of an aged Asian, more grey than brown. He looked not so much frightened as expertly coiled into a shape of least resistance. He disappeared behind a spillage of the crowd. She focussed on one or two of the crowd itself. A heavy, bearded black had linked arms with a much slighter white man. In his other arm the black man held a pole with a torn banner attached to it, in the position of a lance. The white man was wearing glasses, and looked like a school-teacher. She was surprised that someone should wear glasses on an occasion like this. Both of them were opening and closing their mouths in time with the deafening and still incomprehensible noise. She found it impossible to associate the mild-looking, bespectacled little man with the rhythmic violence that pounded the air.

The driver's window was again blocked by a policeman's blue coat, but this time the top half of the policeman's body remained invisible. On the right hand side of their line of traffic they could see nothing but policemen's coats, and helmets, and occasionally a tense, expectant face. Although they could not see beyond the line of policemen, they had the feeling that another crowd had formed on the far side of the road.

The gold ring bit more deeply into the girl's wrist. The desire that had been impelling their imaginations beyond the car's progress towards the bed in the seaside town had drained out of them both. "Oh love, what's going to happen, we're in the middle of it."

"We've just got to sit it out."

To his surprise he had difficulty articulating the words. He felt that all the blood-vessels in his throat were swollen, that his blood was surging up into his head, to the rhythm of the chant, faster than the vessels could cope with. He was dizzy and sickeningly hot.

He closed his eyes.

His bride tried to fill her mind with the sweet, comforting pain in her wrist, but kept her eyes open. The next moment the formations of demonstrators and police had dissolved and and the car was being pounded not with sound-waves but with bodies. The mild-looking man in spectacles was leaning over the bonnet of their car, two policemen had hold of him, his face was thumped against the windscreen and held there, distorted, the glasses broken, the nose pressed sideways, lips flattened against teeth as if they would split. He was held there for an eternity while she tracked the slow-motion arrival of a scream.

Her scream split his head, already distended by the now shapeless criss-cross competing chants, her body arrived against his as if thrown from a distance and he convulsively flung her back, the thud of her body against the door coinciding with a renewed crack of the bespectacled man's head on the windscreen. He opened his eyes to see broken glasses and blood-threaded hair, then one of the policemen went limp as a man in denims brought down a long pole on what could only be his neck. The man in glasses wriggled with surprising agility out of the other policeman's relaxed grasp and disappeared into the crowd.

The bride remained crumpled against the door in the position in which she had hit it. She could not focus on what had just happened. She thought that one of these demented people must somehow have forced his way into the car. The car lurched to one side and the other as waves of bodies broke against it. For a passage that neither of them would ever be able to measure the couple neither spoke nor moved. They felt as if they were inside a bubble in the midst of a thick, turbulent fluid.

After a portion of disordered time the front line of the battle, which had been the line of traffic in which they were sitting, seemed to have moved elsewhere. Scattered outriding fights cartwheeled up and down the road. The police had moved on and now for the first time they saw the opposing demonstrators together. A man in a shiny blue suit, with an open-necked shirt, seemed to be trying to force a bearded man's body through the wall of the cinema. The window through which the girl had seen the old man's face was broken, and the same face was looking out again, crying. The words WOG SHIT, in red paint, had appeared on the wall beside the window.

The car in front of them was still stationary. The young man got out and looked at his own car. There was a dent in the offside wing and some paint had been chipped off. He could not believe that so little damage had been done. While he looked at his car the traffic ahead began to move, but not the car in front. He stepped forward and saw that the windscreen had been shattered. The driver, white-faced, was holding a towel around his hand. He wanted to offer help but was dumb. Stepping back to his own car he saw that the windscreen was smeared with blood and there were splinters of glass on the wiper blades. He did not clean the windscreen but got back in the car, started the engine, and pulled out into the middle of the road.

With the car's lurch into movement his wife felt a throb in her wrist. Looking at it she saw a small, crescent-shaped, intense purple bruise.

Her husband drove with his attention fixed on the traffic ahead. He could not stop his foot from trembling on the accelerator. For the whole journey he felt as though he were driving over broken glass.

Going For Walks With Johnno

Other guys were decent to me later, but Johnno was decent when it counted, so he was always special.

As school debuts go, mine must have been close on unique. All the way on the bus, I kept my right arm well down into my trouser pocket. Not what you're thinking. I still had it there as I walked into the classroom and stood in front of the teacher.

"You don't talk to me with your hands in your pockets."

"No, sir."

"Well, then?"

Pause.

"It's not a hand, sir."

This was true.

"Don't smart-arse me, boy. What the devil else would you have on the end of your arm?"

"A hook, sir."

He tapped my upper arm with a ruler, and said, "Out."

Thirty pairs of eyes bored into my back as I slowly withdrew my arm and held up my hook for inspection. There was a pindrop silence, punctuated by a puking noise somewhere to the rear.

By midday, my hook was all round the school. Outside in the yard, people were queuing for tickets to see it, but the kids in my own form said it made them throw up just to look at it, so would I kindly take my dinner and sit in the locker room or they would find themselves unable to eat their own.

I had just got the lid off my lunchbox when a crowd of big guys came shouldering in and said, where was the kid with the hook?

You get used to the predictable comments. But I wasn't ready for what happened next.

"How does it stay on?"

"With straps."

"Take it off."

"I can't, without undressing."

Next thing I know, they've ripped the shirt off me and are starting on my trousers to see if I've got hooks anywhere else. Unfortunately, four guys at once is a bit more than I can handle. Having got me fairly comprehensively stripped, they scatter my sandwiches around the room, stamp on them, twist my good arm behind my back and then tell me to pick them up again.

I am not feeling at all good about this, when suddenly the door flings open and a big tall strong-looking guy comes in. There is instant silence. He is obviously a teacher except that he is in school uniform.

"Names?" he says, and these guys stand there like mice and tell him.

"Next guy clobbers this kid, gets ten," he says. "Beat it."

"What's getting ten?" I ask, when they have all gone.

"They know; you needn't. Get dressed and come with me."

I walk along in silence, half a step behind him. Finally, I risk it.

"I hope you don't mind me asking, but who are you?"

"Just call me Johnno."

"Where are we going?"

"Canteen. Get you some dinner."

"But I've no money."

"You can pay me back."

It turns out he is my friendly neighbourhood form prefect, which we did not have at my previous. They seem to be a special feature of the Grammar.

In the canteen, we buy various things. People stare or nudge their neighbours. Sensing disaster, Johnno says maybe he should carry my tray, which actually I would be glad of, but I say Thank you, I will do it myself. He sits and watches while I eat. Afterwards, we leave together, and he says he will see me around.

"What's getting ten?" I ask various people, but either they don't know or they are not saying.

Next day dinner hour, I am in exile again, and not feeling too good. But at least today I have the right-coloured blazer. I eat one or two sandwiches, and leave the rest. Suddenly, Johnno is there in the locker room.

"Why are you sitting out here again?"

"The other kids still say it makes them throw up. You can't blame them."

"You've every right to sit in there."

"It's O.K. I'll just kick around."

"No you won't. You'll walk into Town with me."

"There's no need. Really."

"Yes, there is. I know. We'll walk into Town every day for a week if need be; or as long as it takes."

As we set out, I shove my arm deep down in my pocket.

"Take it out," says Johnno. "Do you want people to think you can't let it alone?"

"I don't care what they think."

"Then why are you hiding it?"

"People don't like to see it."

"They'll just have to put up with it. You're going to walk into Town beside me with both arms swinging."

I am not too keen, but somehow it is better than I expected.

"We have gone a little way in silence when Johnno says, "I'll tell you something for nothing. You'll know it sooner or later so it may as well be now. Anne Boleyn was born with an extra finger."

This revelation seems somewhat inconsequent. "So?", I venture at last.

"So, somewhere down the line to make things all square, somebody had to end up with one too few."

He holds out his left hand. It is perfectly shaped and all correct in every way, except there are only three fingers.

"I hadn't even noticed."

"Does it bother you to look at it?"

"No, why should it? It's different, but it's O.K."

"That's the way it has to be with your hook."

A bit later, he asks me if I am having any more trouble with the older guys, and crossing my fingers I tell him no. It is not a very big lie, as it hasn't been as bad yesterday. I notice his lips suddenly tighten.

"There's one thing. Don't let them make you play Pass the Parcel."

"What's that?"

"You know the kids' game? Whoever's got it when the music stops begins tearing off the wrappings. Winner gets whatever's inside."

"But I could easily manage one-handed."

He gives me a strange look. "Don't be a prick."

"I don't understand then."

"You'd be the parcel."

"Oh. I see."

We walk on a little way in silence.

"Happened to me once in the First Year. Not nice. The guy was killed later on his motorbike, and I was glad. Not very Christian, I'm afraid, but there it is."

I do not at all like to think of this thing happening to Johnno. From his expression, I sense that he has let out more than he meant. There is an awkward pause, and then he goes on quickly.

"Anyway, I doubt if they'll try it. You might put your hook somewhere they wouldn't want. But I promise you, if anyone lays a finger on you, I'll take them apart."

"Thanks; I can look after myself."

"Sure. Like yesterday dinner-time."

No comment.

"There's times when a kid needs back-up. Any kid. It's nothing to be ashamed of. It's not easy changing schools mid-term, never mind the hook. But if you've got somebody better in mind, that's up to you."

This hurts, because I am beginning to get a very good feeling about him.

"No, Johnno, no one. Honestly."

"Why say Honestly? Either speak the truth and leave it at that, or keep your mouth shut."

There are too many people on the pavement. To avoid a head-on collision when we all absurdly side-step in the same direction, Johnno steers me for a moment, placing his arm across my shoulder. Normally I have this thing about being handled – ask anyone in care – but today surprisingly I find I have no objection.

On Wednesday, as we walk into Town, Johnno says abruptly, "You're still up at Pelham House, are you?"

"No. Not any more. They just put me there for a month or two to begin with."

"Fostered, then?"

"Yes. Anyway, how did you know?"

"They always seem to be called 'House' these Council places; Pelham House, Chatham House, Wellington House." As if he's counting memories on his fingers.

"You too?"

"For a while. I lodge at my grandad's now."

Lodge? But the matter is not pursued. Instead, Johnno asks what I think of my teachers.

"Not a lot. I like the Maths man. He's the only one who doesn't try to make silly jokes like where's my parrot."

"That'll be Prince."

"No. Some other name. I've forgotten."

"The kids call him Prince. Short for Prince Charming."

"Oh." I feel vaguely uncomfortable without knowing why.

"First lesson he ever taught here, fifth form, Prince comes into the room to find a half-unrolled rubber draped artistically across the centre of his desk, very much used. Nobody admits ownership, so Prince whips out a ruler and says: Right lads, Cinderella principle; line up against the wall and get 'em off; then we can see who it fits. Classic."

"What happened then?"

"History doesn't relate," says Johnno. "Supply your own ending. Same with all the best stories."

I am not too sure I agree, but I don't like to say so. In any case, I am still wondering how Johnno knows so much about me. However, mention of History reminds me, some guys had said they would be giving me a History test and I had better know the answers; so I take the opportunity to ask Johnno for any suggestions. He says he will tell me the standard catch questions, or as many as he can remember.

"Won't they be annoyed if I know all the answers, though?"

"Probably. But if you know them, you can decide which ones to not-know, and that's better than not knowing."

Having eventually disentangled this, I marvel in silence at Johnno's wisdom.

Next morning, I hit a real low. No History test after all, but in the yard at Break some berk cracks the one about me not scratching my balls with the wrong hand. It is so stale it wouldn't generally bother me; but today I am just somehow not in the mood. My response is probably unwise in view of our respective sizes, and it leads to a series of events which I will not describe, but which culminate in my spending the rest of the morning in the toilets.

At dinner time I am still in there, thinking it would be nice if I could get back cerain useful things like parents and a right hand, but failing these I will settle for weedkiller. Suddenly I hear clackety steel-tipped footsteps approaching, sharply purposeful through the mixed noise. I recognise them immediately as Johnno's.

"Come out of there."

This I will not do. No one is going to see me with my face wet, especially not Johnno. Besides, earlier on, some other kids have seen fit to remark that I needn't think Johnno would be interested in anyone like me; he is merely doing his job. The obvious truth of this does not help. So I tell him to piss off, he doesn't have to be sorry for me; plus one or two equally hostile suggestions. For one tense moment he seems about to break the door down; then I hear him turn with a scrape of his heels and walk away. The minute he is gone, I regret it: maybe I half wanted him to come in and get me.

So today there is no walk. In any case, when I finally emerge, it is raining.

Being Thursday, it is our afternoon for Games, which I am not allowed in case I should do somebody a mischief, so I am sent to the Library which is full of big guys working with their heads down. To my relief they completely ignore me. In between counting the cracks in the ceiling, I realise that three tables away from me is Johnno, writing out of several very large books. I am surprised to see he is wearing spectacles, which I did not know. When he looks up, we elaborately do not notice each other.

After forever, the bell rings, which is a third of the afternoon gone, and all but three of the guys get up and leave. Johnno, I notice with relief, is still there; although I have treated him like shit and dare not look him in the face, I suddenly realise that if he had gone it would have felt very bad indeed. Actually, I would quite like to move closer, though without him knowing.

Leaving his books, he comes across to me, and I silently pray to sink through the floor; which is not granted.

"Walk?"

"What, now?"

He nods. "If you like."

"But haven't you got lessons?"

However, it turns out that as he is in the VI Form, he plans his own time.

"It's raining though."

"No. It's stopped. Anyway, so what?"

While he is packing up his books, I glance down at his work which I am sure must be very good. He has done most of a page, in strong neat handwriting, but I only have time to read the title: To What Extent are Insects Conscious of Their Own Existence?

I cannot see how I will ever manage when it is my turn to write this essay.

Leaving the school gates, we unexpectedly turn towards the country instead of into Town. Johnno is not saying anything, so I just pad along beside him, waiting to get told off. Now and then, cars splash past through the puddles, but most of the time it is just the two of us, pacing along the empty road in the after-rain. When we have gone about half a mile and still Johnno hasn't said anything, I realise he isn't going to. We shall just keep walking in peaceable silence side by side, as if I were a human being. I could do with it going on for a very long time.

After maybe two miles, Johnno finally speaks.

"Do you get around much with the other kids?"

I shrug, and raise the hook slightly.

"That's just an excuse. Once you stop bothering about it, so will they. You ought to go out more."

"Like where?"

"Do you want to come round to my place, Saturday?"

"Why? What for?"

"Chance to get out from under. Talk. Shoot your mouth off about the general bloodiness of life." He hesitates. "Or we could do anything else you might happen to fancy."

I can sense him glancing down at me to find out if he's getting there, and I stare back in total disbelief. "What, hook and all?"

"Why not?"

"It turns people off."

"Not me."

"What are you, then, some sort of freak?"

"Only this." His hand.

We walk on, but it is no longer a good silence, and I wonder why the hell I ever said it. After quite a long way, I just stop dead, eyes down. Not realising, he goes on two or three more paces; then turns round, waiting. It is still a long time before I can get the words out. Several times they come all the way up into my mouth and then slip back down again.

"I'm sorry, Johnno."

Our eyes meet for a few seconds, testing each other across the gap. After a brief pause, he nods, and we walk on.

To change the subject, I ask if he has done O Levels, though to be honest I am not entirely clear what these are.

A little later, I mention casually that I wish I was a crab because their claws grow again if they get bitten off.

"I don't go much on crabs."

"Not that mine was bitten," I add hastily.

He stops, turning to face me. "I'm not bothered about what, or when, or how, or why. You'll do fine, just as you are."

His hair is long at the back, and pussycut at the front. It's the style. For some reason, I very much want to touch it.

"Can I?" I ask.

I think tomorrow I will go out and get mine done the same.

Soon after this, Johnno looks at his watch and we have to turn back. But it is O.K.; because it feels as if we are still going on.

Sue Wilsea

End Of The World

I came to think of the February half-term as an eyesore on the year's landscape, unlike the October week from which one looked down on the glittering lights of the festivals or the May week which sat comfortably in the warm valley between Spring and Summer. Squatting on a piece of waste land, part of Winter but stripped of the latter's seductive camouflage, I saw it as a time when the New Year resolutions had long since been buried and hard unbroken earth stretched ahead as far as the eye could see. Already a stunted month, the holiday foreshortened it even further; it was a time of locked gates, boarded-up shop fronts and 'Open Again at Easter' signs, a closed down time.

Our second year we spent that particular week with friends of yours in a ramshackle cottage at Spurn Point, a long spit of land which narrows and narrows until its tip, like a dragon's tail, curls and dips into the North Sea – 'The End of the World' as you jokingly termed it. Year after year great chunks of shingle and sand were being swallowed up by the sea, I remember you telling me, and eventually the whole Point would become a number of separate islands. I remember you telling me a lot of things – about geography (your subject), teaching, children, politics, life in general. I, younger, coming to the North for the first time into my first teaching job, seemed to know so little. You held me cupped in the palm of your hand and your voice completely filled the space around me like the booming of the waves and the growling of the wind outside the cottage at night. I could not help but listen.

The so-called cottage was little more than a hut with stone floors, an open range and one outside rusted-up tap. It was achingly cold. The front door didn't seal properly and sand blew in even when it was closed. It settled in the food and inside our clothes. But we made light of the hardships, swept and reswept the floors and rubbed at our gritty eyes until they were puffy and pink. We walked for miles, crouched in reeds waiting to spot and photograph different sea-birds, threw pebbles into the hissing sea and stubbed toes and grazed hands clambering over the wet rocks. At night we cocooned ourselves in sleeping bags, swollen green caterpillars, and only touched fingers before we went to sleep – just like a married couple you said, and I pretended not to mind, thinking it was enough that we were together. In the same way I pretended not to mind how the lack of warmth or comfort served to emphasise the distance between us, the chasm of ice that gaped increasingly wider. I was a good actress despite being an indifferent Drama teacher. I masked the fact that I preferred hot, steamy atmospheres – reading in front of a fire, blotching first one, then the other side of my pale flesh or sitting crowded into a corner of a smoke and music filled pub feeling squeezed of air. That's why the only time I liked the school was in winter when the windows had misted up and the smell of bodies hung dank 'and fetid in the gloom of late afternoon. Making love was best those times when we thrashed about in the coarse sheets of that cheap hotel, making them damp with our glistening flesh, and afterwards, unable to open the window which had jammed, fugging the room with cigarette smoke. You preferred the outside; I could always smell it on your clothes and in the salty roughness of your beard. You had to look forward, outward, while my instinct was to crawl back and huddle, embryonic, parasitically, inside myself.

I have some photos. One was taken of the two of us, unawares, as we trudged side by side through the sand-dunes and tall grasses; bent against the wind, our hair and coats streaming behind us, you have your hands deep in your pockets and are gazing directly ahead. My head is slightly turned towards you and a strand of hair has whipped across my face. I have another one of you, alone, on the shore-line holding a piece of white driftwood like a huge bleached bone; behind you the backcloth of grey sea and sky is seamless. And there's one of me, perched on a rusty oil-drum, determinedly smiling to the camera, only later noticing the brown marks like old blood-stains on the seat of my clothing. Later, I would scrutinise these photos minutely for signs, expressions, signals that I had failed to notice at the time.

You went back to your wife shortly afterwards and I wasn't really surprised. At least you never pretended, either to her or to me, to be anything other than you were although I hadn't realised I was not the first to have been taken to the Point to mark the final act of the play. That element of stage management in what had appeared so natural did hurt, hurt badly. I decided to expose my wounds to the open air rather than, as I'd always done before, binding them tightly with layers of self-deception. They were raw and stung, especially that time I met the two of you with the children all out shopping together, or when I noticed you talking to my replacement in the staffroom while she looked up at you in a way that was so familiar it was like holding up a magnifying glass to my pain.

I left at the end of the summer term and for the first time in my life felt as though I had stopped trying to follow timetables that had been devised by others. For the moment, there was no future and thus the linear concept of time was meaningless. I tore up the calendar and carefully packed away my clocks, wristwatch and diary. I lived in the present, which was as short or long as that particular second, minute, hour or day seemed to be. Sometimes I would pick at the scabs of my resentment, making them bleed afresh, but of course, in time, they did heal and the seal of new skin was tougher than before. February passed almost without my noticing it.

In the Spring I arranged to stay in the cottage once more, this time by myself. It was still as bleak and cold as I'd remembered but by then it didn't matter. I'd adapted, both in the practical sense by bringing with me draught excluders, heaters, a stove, extra blankets and clothing and within myself too. At last, I could distinguish between what was really me and what was external and maintain some kind of balance. You were wrong, you see, wrong about so many things, not least about mentally dividing up time and yourself. Both are too precious, too much of a complex intricately-worked mosaic, to be hacked into pieces. The important thing to do is to live in the moment, not outside it. Time will just flow on regardless. like the water round the Point, so you might as well be swept along together. And you were mistaken about Spurn – it *is* being eroded but it reforms itself too – certainly it will never break up into the archipelago of your imagination.

It and I will both survive. In fact, if you walk along the shore in the early morning you can just about see the South Bank when the shroud of mist lifts. It doesn't feel like the end of the world anymore – more like the beginning.

Justice

It took us four and a half weeks to drive overland from England to Pakistan, that homeland of my ancestors. We had adventures, of sorts, along the way. My biggest memory is of the incident at the border post between Turkey and Iran. We did not have such a good time there.

It was my father's idea for us to go overland. He said that although it would take longer it would work out much cheaper than flying. As a few of my uncles were also going, father decided that it would be 'good business' to buy some vans – we would be able to sell these at double or triple the price in Pakistan; Inshalla. Father is always hitting upon money spinning scemes like that; the Big Businessman, my father is. Or so he loves to think. It is a sad fact that he made a blunder in coming to the gold paved streets of Britain to make his fortune, because he never did. However his brothers, who we stayed with in Pakistan, remained in Lamahbad, on the Indus, and there they have made quite a fortune. They now own a marble quarry, a mine, and have a big stake in the local chemical fertilizer industry. Compared to us they live in the greatest luxury, and my father is shamefaced about this. Although he loves his hometown of Lamahabad "to the dust of its streets" he refuses to settle back there until he has made a fortune for his family. So, weather permitting, it looks as though he will see his last sunset in Millbridge, England.

We began the journey from Milbridge in a small convoy of four blue ford transit vans. My father, me, and my mother were in one van, various uncles and relations in the others. All the vans were chock-a-block with goods that my father and uncles considered to be investments; things that would sell well in Pakistan, Turkey or Iran, or that would at least make good presents for family.

We were in high spirits when we set off, waved and cheered by our friends. Mother was weeping. She had roasted a dozen chickens that were supposed to be our food supplies through Europe – there would be no halal meat until Turkey. Having heard that the water in Turkey and Iran was not so good she also stocked up with bottles of fizzy lemonade. Much as I love her it must be said that my mother lacks a certain sense of 'reality'; the chickens lasted as far as Germany, and nobody wanted to drink the lemonade. It was her lack of sense of 'reality' that landed us in the trouble in Iran.

Although we crossed deserts where even camels lay dead from the heat and where white bones littered the landscape as far as the eye could see; edged along hazardous ledges where the earth plunged away into bottomless ravines; saw fabulous lakes and jewels of sunsets which were beautiful beyond singing of them; for me the best part of the journey was travelling through Austria. The scenery of that country is so wonderful, and the people treated us with respect; as equals.

As I have already said the worst part of the journey was at the border post between Turkey and Iran.

Here we had lost track of two of the vans, and were to meet up later with them, in Tehran. In the van following ours was Uncle Habib, his close friend Mohammed, and a boy younger than me, Sadiq. Uncle Habib and Mohammed were an odd couple to be the greatest of friends; Habib talks constantly and about anything, whereas Mohammed rarely speaks at all. Sadiq, a frail and goof-teethed child, was a wimp.

The problems at the border post began with the passports. We all handed over our Pakistan passports, apart from mother. She was, for some reason, chin-up back-straight proud of her dark blue British passport. Despite warnings from Habib and Mohammed, who had made this journey before, she absolutely refused not to show it to the Iranian border guards. Mother's passport had a funny effect upon the guard who collected it from her. He was a young man, early twenties, with a devout Muslim beard and a gleam of fervour in his bright eyes. After opening mother's passport he screamed with rage and threw it violently to the ground, spitting after it, then flooding out a fountain of most un-holy curses upon my father and mother. We were all out of the vans, stretching our limbs, and I, dutiful son, recovered the passport from the dusty ground. The young guard rewarded me with a mighty slap across my head that set my ears ringing. As if from the cracks in the ground more guards appeared, scowling as they pointed automatic rifles at us, clicking off the safety catches. We all froze, rigid with fear, for although most of these guards were very young their eyes were harsh stones; death was nothing to them. To them people were as flies.

We were made to line up in the glare of the sun, away from the shade of the vans. Rifles were trained on us while the guards ransacked the vans, scattering our belongings over the ground. I could see that Sadiq was trembling, close to tears, but I stood proud, if a little foolish, with my ringing head.

The young guard who had taken the passports seemed to be in command at the post. He went away to a brick hut and began shrieking into a telephone in rapid Arabic. Mother's blue passport lay where it had been slapped from my hand, discarded in the red dust, the boot print of a border guard stamped onto its cover.

When the young guard stormed back from the hut he picked up the passport between thumb and forefinger, holding it out away from himself as though it was made of fresh turd. He ordered us all into one van, ours, then father was told to drive into the centre of the compound yard. The yard was closed in by brick walls, with a green doored and shuttered barrack hut running down one side. At the corner of the barrack hut and one wall stood a tin roofed shelter, and in the shade of this shelter was a large red clay water urn. Father was made to park in the centre of the yard, away from any shade, and we were told that we had to stay in the van until our passports and documents had been cleared with a central office. There was no answer when we asked how long all this would take. Instead we were told that there was a good chance of us all being arrested as British spies; we would be tortured; we would be flogged; if we were lucky we would be executed outright.

We endured many such threats from the boy-guards that day. Habib put their malice down to the fact that they had not been selected to die on The Front with so many thousands of their brothers, but instead had been sent to this forsaken forgotten border post. They had to prove their worth somehow, and insulting guests to their country seemed to be the way that they had chosen. Of course Habib did not say this to the boy-guards themselves; even Habib respects silence when confronted with a loaded rifle.

In the back of the van it was hot. Father began nagging at mother for bringing such trouble upon us with her foolish misplaced pride, but in the presence of Habib and Mohammed mother stayed respectfully silent and aloof. Eventually father ceased in his nagging; it was too hot to moan about anything for too long.

We all fell silent and drowsy. It was so hot in that airless van. The metal walls were hot to touch. We had to cram in the shade, all of us sweating. I think that by the end of the day the heat had cooked our brains and sent us all a little funny in the head.

Habib, never one for an excess of silence, began telling his stories. Like a lot of people from Pakistan he is a great believer in things supernatural, and so he told us again of his encounter with the woman who glowed green.

One night, in his youth in Lamahbad, he was returning home from the mosque. Allowing haste to overcome fear he decided to take a short-cut past the cemetery. Lying stark naked on the cemetery wall beneath a tall tree was a beautiful young woman, surrounded by a halo of green glowing light. A goddess. Habib approached her, hoping to take advantage of her nakedness. Stunned by her beauty he bent over her face to steal a kiss. Without once opening her eyes she placed her hand gently on his chest and pushed lightly. That push sent him flying through the air and he was caught in the uppermost branches of the tree. Shrieking in panic he tumbled down from the tree and rushed away toward the town, the lady still lying naked and serene upon the wall.

Habib tells it better than I can, and swears by Allah that it is true. My father says that in those days Habib was a fiend for whisky and hashish, and that this may be something to do with his recollections of that night.

Seeing us distracted from the heat by his storytelling Habib went on to tell us about the wild bandits who had chased him across Afghanistan; about the motorcyclist he had seen flogged in Tehran for driving through the streets in a T-shirt; about the injured lamb that when picked up by his father had turned into a demon-woman...

On and on he talked. Eventually he was hoarse through talking.

"Give me some water; this storytelling has given me a raving thirst."

"There is no water," mother said. "Only that fizzy lemonade there."

She pointed to the last of the plastic lemonade bottles, jammed between the front seats of the van.

"Pah! A man cannot drink that." Habib crouched up in the van, peering through the open window. He was eyeing across the corner where the clay urn stood. We had seen soldiers dipping a metal cup into the urn and then drinking in long slow gulps, looking over with smiling eyes to the van. Habib called for the guards to bring some water, but there were now no guards to be seen, and nobody answered his shouts. Habib climbed from the van, stretched like a cat in the sun, then went striding boldly across the yard toward the water urn. His footsteps scuffed in the sand, and before he was half way across the yard a guard came leaping from the shadows of the barrack wall, jabbing his rifle toward Habib, screaming at him to get back into the van or die.

"But we need water," Habib croaked, thumbing toward the urn to make his meaning clear. The guard clicked the safety-catch off on his rifle, and from the glare of his eyes it looked as though it needed only another stride from Habib to set the bullets raining.

"We need water. By the mercy of Allah, water." More guards

appeared from the shadows, rifles pointing at Habib and the van. Habib sighed toward the sky, bowed his submission, then returned to the van in quick short strides, muttering foul curses for all to hear. He climbed back into the van and slammed the door. Mother offered him the lemonade bottle, but he refused it with a sharp wave, then drew his knees to his chest, crouching into a sulk. The rest of us drank gladly from the bottle, but the lemonade was sweet and warm, leaving us as thirsty as ever. Eventually Habib succumbed and took a long drink from the bottle. As we were drinking a boy-guard appeared grinning in the van window, watching us. He was no older than me, fourteen at that time, and he was trying hard to grow a beard. He looked silly, but dangerous.

"Hey, you there," he snapped at Mohammed. "Give me the English cigarettes." With a rifle barrel he jabbed toward the Benson and Hedges packet that lay on the rug between Mohammed and my father. Now we all knew that these were Mohammed's last packet of English cigarettes; the way he had been treasuring them for days had become a joke with us. He was trying to spin them out so that he could avoid the local cigarettes, which he claimed were as harsh as wood shavings on the throat.

"Quickly; give me them, or die."

Mohammed studied the cigarette packet, then looked up at the boy, then back to the packet. After a long pause he slowly reached out and lifted the packet, took out a single cigarette, and offered it across to the boy.

"No. Give me them all, or die."

But Mohammed just gazed into the boy's eyes, then through him with a far-away stare, placing the cigarette between his own lips, his eyes never once leaving the boy's. The cigarette looked very small and very white against the background of his coarse black beard.

"For the love of Allah, and for the sake of my van, give him the cigarettes," my father muttered. Father and Habib were sweating. Only Mohammed looked cool. He produced a cigarette lighter, flicked at it with his thumb, and lit the cigarette in a single puff. Little Sadiq was sitting behind Mohammed, his face stiff with fear. The safety-catch on the gun clicked. As the boy-guard scowled Mohammed calmly blew a steady stream of smoke toward him, then again offered out the cigarette. Silence gripped us all in the stomach, the hum of the flies seeming louder, louder. Then the boy-guard laughed and his face broke warm, tinkling out merry curses as he staggered away from the van. There were sighs all round the van, except from Mohammed, and even my father lit up a cigarette, his hands trembling.

A nervous silence followed, all of us staring at the cigarettes on the rug, my mother clucking and tutting.

"If I were a wise man," Mohammed said, considering the lit end of his cigarette, "I would have given that little no-beard my stupid cigarettes. But Pride is a great failing in me. So foolish. And I, who have seen these people and their so called justice before. I could easily have died for those cigarettes."

"Well, of course they do say that cigarettes are dangerous for the health," cracked Habib. We all laughed. Sadiq grinned goofily at me, and I twitched back a smile; brothers in misfortune.

"So, and what of their justice?" my father said to Mohammed.

"Yes," Habib said. "Kill more time. Tell us your traveller's tale about their justice. My throat and stories are all dried out."

Mohammed pulled hard on his cigarette, his eyes swinging over to Habib.

"No traveller's tale Habib; this is true. As true as we all sit here frying. It happened the last time that I came overland to Pakistan; two years ago, and with your own cousin, Uzmat. No doubt you have heard of this from his lips."

Mohammed, who had swollen to take on heroic proportions in my estimation, carefully stubbed his cigarette on the wall of the van.

"That time we also passed through Iran because Afghanistan was closed. We were almost through Iran and had come upon no trouble. In fact most of the people were very friendly, and we often ate without being charged. Now, perhaps, things are different; the land was not at war then. So, we were almost at the Pakistan border. It was mid-day, very hot, water mirages shimmering over the distant flat sands, making mountains appear to be islands floating in the sky. We came upon a car that had skidded off the road and had crashed into the only tree for miles around. An unbelievable misfortune; that driver must have been ill-fated. One side of the car was smashed, all buckled, and huddled into the tiny shade of the tree stood a veiled woman. She was wailing, face in her hands. The guards were also there with their rifles and their landrover. They made us pull over, and without any explanation ordered us to take the woman and her belongings into our van, and take her across the border. We were not ones to argue with guns; not so close to home. The woman was wailing, beyond words. Crying all the time; all the way. Beside the crashed car stretched out in the sand, were the bodies of two men. Both were bloody and plagued with flies; we presumed that they had been her travelling companions; that they had died in the crash. We waited until we were in Pakistan before asking the woman to explain what of the car. The passenger was his uncle. They had been tired; driving since dawn; the heat; the dust. The car had skidded from the road and hit the tree, killing the husband's uncle in the passenger seat. The woman, in the back, had been unhurt. Her husband had shock, but no serious damage. After a while the guards in their landrover came along the road. The husband flagged them down and explained what had happened. But the guards had no sympathy. They said that a death in their country could not be passed off without official investigation. The guards stepped away and whispered in consultation. When they came back it was with grim faces. "Justice has to be done," they had said. And those guards, in their lawful powers, decreed that due to his careless driving the woman's husband had been responsible for the death of his passenger. Accordingly, as was law, life had to be paid for with life; a death for a death. And so, right there on the spot, before his own wife's eyes, they had executed him. She said that they shot him through the head before he even realised what was happening. He never even had a chance to plead for mercy.

Yes, if my senses were with me I would have given that no-beard my stupid cigarettes."

"Oh, more, more," Habib jeered when Mohammed had finished. "Cheer our hearts with your little travel stories."

"It is true," was all that Mohammed would say, and then he leaned back against the hot van wall with his eyes closed, as if sleeping on his own heavy thoughts. Mohammed's story had shocked me. Shocked us all. It made us gloomy again, and I think we were all fearing for our lives.

For over eight hours they kept us couped up in the heat of that van. Not until the day began to cool into evening did the young guard in charge return with our documents and mother's passport.

"You can go now," he growled. "But next time, do not bring such piles of filth with you." He jabbed a finger at mother's passport, then strode away toward the barracks.

We were out of that hell-hole within minutes, not even waiting to inspect the damage to our belongings, or to even ask for food and water. The guards were washing in preparation for the evening prayers. Some of them waved, as if to departing relatives, as we drove away in clouds of red dust.

We were two months in Pakistan.

At the end of that time we flew home to England, and once again my mother proudly showed her dark blue passport, although this time without incident.

Heaven And The Have Nots

Florence Binney was born in Gateshead in the year 1900.

She had taken to thinking of both the town and the twentieth century as her own and had never hoped to live outside the boundaries of either. Not that she ignored matters of a more international nature: she had been particlularly upset over the Second World War. But that was something else again.

Flo had believed for many years that she would live to within a heartbeat of the next century – old age and illness appearing feeble adversaries in comparison to the poverty and tribulations that had come before. The gloomy faces now gathered around her bedside forced her to acknowledge alternatives. They were digging her grave with their wan smiles and benevolent whispers.

Especially that Doris Dribble.

Doris was wittering by the bedside. Flo could make out the top of her small wrinkled head which was almost level with the covers. It wasn't that Doris was particularly short, or sitting, or bowed down. The reason Doris could hardly be seen was the height of the bed. Flo had in her more mature years taken greater care of her virginity than she had when it was more likely to be threatened and had raised the bed on bricks till it was over five feet from the ground. She told everyone that this was a deterrent to the casual rapist and that it also saved on fuel bills as heat had an uncommon tendency to rise.

The doctor was by the curtained window leafing through a three month old copy of Family Friend and waiting for the kettle to boil. Doris went over and pulled at his sleeve.

"Will it be long? Will it take much longer, doctor?"

"No, it's nearly boiling now, Mrs Dribble."

"I don't mean the tea, doctor! I mean Flo! Will she have to suffer much longer?"

The doctor was puzzled.

"I don't think she is suffering, Mrs Dribble. She'll be feeling a little weak of course. I think it may be something to do with having to climb the rope ladder to get into bed. (She really should get herself a proper ladder, you know!) But there's no reason to believe she'll die. She can get over this."

But death had got a foothold somewhere in the room, for surely it was there, in the bedroom where the one bar electric fire singed the dust that swam between stray shafts of sunlight, and crouching dimly in the stairwell hiding from the grey arc of the forty watt bulb.

If you listened carefully you could hear Death whispering in the creaking and trembling of the housejoints at night. Flo listened. Then she would fret and sob about a thousand things that had and had not been. She would fall into sleep unwillingly, for sleep no longer refreshed her, rather it took something from her. She was calmer in her warm bed with her eyes open and a hand clasping the bible. Above the bed was a crucifix made from sea shells which she had bought on a day trip to Whitley Bay fifteen years before. Now she craned her head back to look at it, then raised her bible to read:

> And I saw a new heaven and a new earth
> For the first heaven and the first earth had passed away.

Flo stared at the pale washed ceiling where the rough brush strokes still showed through and tried to dream of heaven. As a child she had mistaken the name 'Heaven' for 'Hebburn', a town further down the River Tyne. It seemed the height of injustice to her childish mind that some people were born in heaven while others had to live honestly and poorly for the whole of their lives to get there. This quibble over divine providence had been further aggravated by the presence of a classmate – Doris, that future Mrs Dribble - whose family had moved to Gateshead from Hebburn. Doris's father was a shopkeeper and the family was well off, in a penny-pinching way. But Doris always came to school with her hair perfectly in place, her dress spotlessly clean and patchless, and always seemed to have a halfpenny for sweets. "Why wasn't I born in Hebburn?" Flo had asked her widowed mother who had shrugged her shoulders and said such things were up to the Council. "What powerful beings the Council must be!" Flo had thought to herself.

Now these same thoughts came back to her. She settled herself comfortably among the boulder-like pillows and began to look forward to heaven. Would God have the kettle on and do they eat biscuits in Heaven? Would the fire be stoked up? Would the kitchen be cosy with the smell of ironing? Would the radio be playing one of her favourites? She was distracted from her daydreams by Doris's whiney voice echoing in the hallway. She was assailing the doctor with an arsenal of trivialities.

"So it's nothing contagious, doctor?"

"Not in the least!" he replied reaching for the doorhandle.

She grabbed his arm.

"It's not me I'm worried about you understand, doctor. But there's others, and what with my little cat, Billy..."

"And there's no chance of your cat going down with anything, Mrs Dribble!" he broke in thickly before levering himself out of the door with a short "Good day!"

Doris went back into the living room to speak with Flo.

"Well they've all gone now Flo and what a time I've had to manage them. I'd better be on my way though before it gets too dark and the streets aren't safe anymore. I'll come and see you later when I've made little Billy something to eat (bless his little heart) and we can watch This is Your Life on the telly."

And then she left. With Doris gone Flo relaxed a little. Theirs was a curious friendship, spanning eighty years. It had been Doris who had approached the other in the rooftop playground, anxious to make a new companion in a new place. She was fingering the ribbon in her hair as if surprised to find it there. Florence was staring at her fluttering hands.

"Do you like my ribbon?" Doris asked

Flo nodded.

"You can have it if you want?"

Flo said nothing, only drew her eyes away to look across the slate rooves down to the river where the cranes swung across the skyline without breath or sound. Doris came so close that her words tickled Flo's ear as she said:

"Here, I've got lots more, I don't mind!"

And she unfurled her hair with an animal innocence and pressed the ribbon into the young girl's slack hand.

When Doris returned home and her mother asked what had happened to the ribbon she told her that Flo had taken it. The next day Doris's mother came to the school and took it back. She called Flo a thief and worse and ended up by losing her temper and slapping her.

That should have been the end of everything but Doris always had a way of making up. She admired Flo, even at so tender an age; she needed her strength, needed her calm, for Doris was one who could only exist through someone else.

But time and time again Doris had reacted against her own weakness and turned upon her friend, sometimes with a spiteful word, or a broken promise, and then as regularly as the seasons, with some premeditated act redolent with malice. Flo had learnt to live with her ways but these little acts of treachery had chipped away at her heart and the love that now remained was only that of familiarity. Doris was a burden, a spiked and barbed companion to be borne with humility. Throughout the long years Doris had been on Flo's doorstep to borrow, to badger, in sickness and in health. "We all have our cross to bear," she would tell herself. "And mine is Doris!"

Then she would ask the Almighty to forgive her for thinking so ill of him—or so well of Doris as to be an emissary of divine intent.

Flo closed her eyes and tried to rest a while before Doris returned. She felt a cold breeze on her cheek and then heard the window panes shuddering. She sat herself up and listened. Doris had left the front door open. Flo cursed her under her breath and flung the bedclothes from her. She began lowering herself off the edge of the bed, turning onto her stomach. There was a cold draught of air on her feet and ankles. She felt dizzy. Pin points of light punctured the air before her eyes. "I'm going to faint." she thought and tried to pull herself back upon the bed. But her strength had left her and she fell and it seemed so strange because it took so long to reach the floor. She lay numbly staring at the ceiling and seeing the rough brushmarks turning into clouds. A gust of wind caught the door and it closed with a crack. Her thin, grey hair danced gently over her brow. The earth shivered and she closed her eyes to dream. Florence Binney passed away as she slept.

When Florence Binney arrived in Heaven she was truly surprised.

She had expected Heaven to be many things, but she had never expected it to be Gateshead, but Gateshead is what it was.

She found herself stepping off the tram in Prince Consort Road. Smiling, vaguely familiar faces passed her on the street and greeted her by name. A neat looking man approached her. He had a pencil thin moustache and carried a sheaf of papers under his left arm. He addressed her formally: "Good day, Mrs Binney, I'm so glad to meet you! I'm Mr Goat of the Celestial and municipal Gateshead Council. We have your new home all prepared. It really isn't far. Do follow me!"

And so she followed him.

It was an autumn morning, crisp as any that had ever been, with a hopelessly blue sky and the tenderest of clouds. Of course it was a different Gateshead to the one she had left. The cobbled streets could have been carved by master masons and the terraced houses mounting the banks were as bright as tropical birds. They walked along Saltwell Road at a brisk pace. She recognized the streets but the names had changed. Gone were Stevenson Street, Arkwright Street and Trevethick Street and in their places were Wilson, Betty and Kepple Street. The cemetery that had once stood by the church had been converted into a ginger biscuit factory. Flo dawdled for a moment, tapping her heels on the cobbles. She looked down at her feet, her small delicate feet. She was wearing buttoned shoes of patent leather and thick lisle stockings. She passed a hand over her cheek to feel the smooth skin. They walked a little further. Mr Goat stopped at the door of 22 Max Bygraves Terrace and pushed it open (for there were no locks on the doors). The first thing Flo noticed was the smell of freshly ironed linen. As she passed the living room she could hear the Mills Brothers singing 'Autumn Leaves' on the radio. The kitchen was neat and warm with a bright, glowing fire. A plate of ginger snaps was waiting on the table and the kettle was just beginning to boil, ready for a cup of tea. Mr Goat explained that the kettle boiled eternally and never needed filling. Among the modern conveniences was a fridge forever stocked with a half pound of cod fillets and a pound of potted meat. In a corner of the larder ready made twists of tea were to be found for anyone who cared to come and borrow them. Mr Goat told Flo that there was always an ample stock of essentials unless you fancied a chat or a cup of tea with one of the neighbours, then the supply of some necessary commodity would dwindle to nothing. It was a masterful piece of organisation and Flo expressed admiration at the efficacy of the arrangement.

"You will be given an allowance to pay for the rent and coal and so forth," continued Mr Goat, "…and if you care to lend a hand at the biscuit factory."

"Naturally, naturally!" Flo enjoindered. "I don't expect to get anything for nothing. I'll do my bit, don't you worry. I wouldn't have it any other way!"

"As we've discovered in the past!" Mr Goat replies agreeably.

He provided Flo with a rent book and left her to settle in.

She went round the house beaming. In the living room she ran her hands lovingly along the velvet curtains and caressed the battalion of chalk and plastic ornaments that crowded the mantlepiece like lemmings. The coal fire blazed cheerfully and the stout sofa and chairs bulged in anticipation of a body to enthrone. The bedroom window looked out on the Teem Valley: rich pasture land turning its face to the sun with a peasant family just then resting from their labours in the shade of an oak. Flo thought she heard a knock at the door and came hurriedly down the stairs. The door stood open but there was no one to be seen. Then she heard movements in the living room and she hurried in. There before the fire was a young woman wearing a cross over pinafore, shyly twisting a strand of her long thick hair between thumb and forefinger. Flo stared without fully understanding.

"It was that damned cat, Flo! I went home and tripped over that damned cat and banged me head on the banister! I was here before you were, which is why I got one of the detached houses up the road, I suppose. Now how about a cup of tea, pet? I'm clean out myself!"

Simon S.S. Says

Simon says: Come…Simon *says*.

I nearly did. I nearly said it. Then she would have had to come. If I said it once. If I said it again. But something in her face said it could not be said. It told me that she would have turned me away, far away. Oh, I did say it once – ever so quietly. But not again. So she did not come and I had to leave her.

I wanted us to be there, we two where the lights go on and on. Where there's lots and lots. But I was afraid to say it again. Afraid for her and afraid for me the branches are shaking in the old peach tree.

I passed her on my way away. I had to go. Time was going swish swish so fast that it was hard even to stop my feet. But I did. She thought it was just like any other time when I stopped in front of Nursie Station B. I'd always stop and stare at her. I'd just have to say it once and *say* it again. Then I could. I knew I shouldn't. Most nursies would tell you to move on. But Simon had said it so there you are.

"Simon says, have a pleasant day, Pinkie." That's what I called her.

"Thank-you, Simon."

"Simon *s-s-says*."

"Well, I'll certainly try, Simon."

I stood staring. A food cart bumped along between us.

"I know where there's more food."

"Mmmm?" She was looking at papers on her desk.

"In the Superstore."

"Very good, Simon. Well said."

"I say a lot m-m-more than that."

"I'm sure you do."

"In my head. There I say it almost smooth. Simon s-says it once. Then Simon says it again and I c-c-c-can do it."

"Very good."

She couldn't look at me anymore. She wanted me to go away. Her pretty head was bent at the neck so she didn't have to see me. Pinkie was fearful. I knew it. Her hair was all smooth and stuck together but there's no telling what it would have done without all that hair spray. I expect it would be flying away still because that's how fearful she was. My face was stubble black. I knew I didn't smell right. My hair had not been brushed. It was all over my face. I scared her from her head to her soul even with the hair spray.

I told my carpet slippers to start moving again. But only the once.
So they stayed and I stayed looking.

I said, "Pinkie, c-c-come." My voice was a little thin wind whistling
in my ears.

She looked up. "Hmmm?"

"...Crumb, I said. Bread crumbs: 28 cents f-for a quarter p-p-
pound."

"Is that right?"

"Y-y-yes..."

Another nursie was at the desk now. She had no eyebrows. None
at all. Only grease brown lines she drew on each day. Pinkie was
talking to her. She was on the chair under those grease brown arches
feeling safer there than looking at me.

Carpet slippers across the floor. Simon *says*. Says it sad. Shuffle
shuffle.

There was a time when I could have said come. Said it once, said
it twice. But time went swish swish and everything was swimming
so I couldn't think:

It was Arts and Crafts. There was our teacher and it was Pinkie's
turn to sit in the chair behind Teacher and keep an eye. But the chair
was empty still. No pink in sight.

Then Pinkie ran in and nearly tripped over Tom's false leg. I could
tell that she wasn't so well. Her all-weather coat was dark with the
soak of the rain and her hair lay in wet, sticky streaks across her
white forehead. She took off her coat. Her crisp blouse had escaped
the tuck of her uniform pinafore, all pink and pin-striped. She *almost*
looked like one of us. And her eyes were all twitchy at the thought
of it.

We were making popsicle stick houses that day. Teacher was going
from table to table, counting in her head everyone's share of sticks
so that her old lips moved silent with the numbers but not so silent
as she thought. Pinkie was looking into a little mirror she took from
her purse and wiping away the little bits of blackness that were
running away from her eyes into the hollows below. But mostly she
was trying to smooth down her hair with a pat here and a pat there.
It was not easy and I knew that in her little mirror she saw her eyes
twitching.

They didn't stop either when she saw Tom scratching his false
leg. Or Emma, the half-dressed school teacher, counting up to thirty-
three with her sticks. I just sat in my little fold-up chair crying.
Crying for the fear of my nursie-girl and her hair that was flying away.

I wanted to say – oh, how badly I wanted to say – poor, poor girl in your pink-striped pinafore, come with me, come to the Superstore.

Yes, come to the Superstore with me.

I wanted to tell her about the shiny gold cans of hair spray, row after row – she'd need worry no more. About the mirrors on the walls behind Fruits & Vegetables where she might forever put herself together. Then there was that music...those little melodies so soft in the back of your ear. They'd make her forget Tom and his itchy plastic leg.

"There's no need," she was saying to Emma who was on number 26. No need at all."

Then she looked at me looking at her and crying. There was the slightest bit of a wrinkle in Pinkie's oh-so-smooth forehead. She knew that I knew. She knew that I knew that she was *this* close to not knowing the Me from the Them. She looked hard into my eyes. Still I wanted to say it's not too late...Not too late to come to the Superstore with me. There's MORE in the Superstore. Not just aisles and aisles but smiles and smiles...

"Why are you crying, Simon?" The pink pinstripes were over me now. You would never have known that anything had ever been crooked. "What do you want?"

"MORE."

"No need to be so emphatic about it, Simon. We don't want to seem rude, do we? I'll bring you more popsicle sticks if that is what you want. Just ask nicely next time, alright?"

She laid a small pile at my side. I was still crying soft tears. And my nose went drip drip. As she bent down to lay the sticks on my side of the table, I reached my hand to her head and touched her hair. It was under control once more. Then she moved her head away from my touch.

"Time to build your house, Simon." Her voice was firm. She had recovered. She knew the Me from the Them again. I was happy even though I knew I could never, never now say come to the Superstore. Never now.

"A store is m-more," was all I could say.

"Whatever you like then. Make whatever you like." She knew that I knew that her eyes went twitchy. She'd never come now; I had to tell myself as much.

And that's why I could only say crumb though I wanted her to come as I stared as I stood as she sat behind Nursie Station B... That's why I had to go alone in the end.

I left Pinkie talking to those twin brown arches as I went all the way to the front door. All the way to on the way…It would be like the other times. I had only to walk out the front swing door – right past the porter whose hat is so big that it tips over his eyes.

I was looking at him and he at me. They had given him another hat and it sat square on his head right over his old steely eyes. They were sharp – sharp like the little silver blades they use in the kitchens. They dig the big black eyes out of the potatoes with those little knives. I tried – tried hard to keep my eyes from going all big and black in the white of my face. But I knew that that was it when the light caught on his eyes.

"Where do you think you're going?"

"To the S-S-Superstore."

"A little shopping to take care of, eh? Well, I'm sure they have all the food you could want right here in The Fairweather Villa. So why don't you just run along like a good fella, eh?"

In my room, I open my window. There is a tiny bit of a courtyard just there with a great knotty peach tree ever out of season. Its branches tangle themselves right in front of my window, that high up they are. At the bottom, there are concrete slabs that surround the peach tree.

They look very hard. Still, I must get to the Superstore.

My leg is through the window. More bone than leg. Must look funny to anyone in the garden taking their morning fruit juice. I put one slippy carpet slipper onto the difficult branch. It twists so much there's no telling what it might do. Brave. Be brave, Simon. Simon *says* be brave. I put all my weight on the branch. It groans like my old grandad when he died last year.

My slippers fly from my feet. I won't look down. That's the trick everyone says. I'm looking straight ahead past the red roof tops where all the families live; homes so square I can almost forget the wild of the unwieldy branches. And there beyond the roof tops and the sprawling silver of the TV antennae, I can see it. The grand neon block letters: SUPERSTORE. Not far now…

Down and down until my toes hit ground and wriggle against the cold of it. I take my slippers from the roots of the old peach tree. It's drizzling and grey. The smell of damp is on the sidewalk, now in my nostrils where the LYSOL still swells. Someone has forgotten to turn off the street lights. They still burn yellow in the grey. No need. I know where I'm going. Just one block, two to go.

Those are faces in the fog of that window. A boy and a girl staring. I want to say, come to the Superstore with me, open twenty-four hours a day. It's always bright in the Superstore. But they are staring at my carpet slippers that go flap against the soles of my feet.

I do not dare.

It's the parking lot and I'm running yellow line after yellow line behind me; yellow lines that stay yellow even in the rain, even after the rain, even after you and me. Running so fast that my slipper is flying into that puddle, black and purple and green with the car grease that floats on top. No matter now that I'm here. I might even get a new one at the Superstore. Anything is possible now.

The doors slide away with my footfall. Just like Open Sesame.

Sesame seed buns: Aisle 4. I just know it.

And there, right there, are the bright candy-red gum machines. I pull out a dime and let it go slip into the machine. I catch the two small squares of chewy pink in both hands. I'm blowing a bubble. "This one's for you, Pinkie." I blow it long and hard so that, for a moment, everything turns a wonderful rose: the shopping carts; the children that cluster around the horse that goes giddy-up for a quarter; even my slipperless foot...

And I'm walking. Walking toward myself who is walking toward me in a little black-and-white TV. I've never been on TV before. Never once before in my life. I'm waving. I'm blowing a bubble bigger than all my face and another that goes pop. I'm walking backwards. All on TV. They think of everything at the Superstore.

Just taking a stroll. Everything is as it should be. I smile at the pretty blonde cashier and she smiles back. Not just aisles and aisles but smiles and smiles. I'm humming along with the tune that drips from the ceiling. Dee da dee da dee da dum...And the light that goes on and on is breaking over every silver tin of soup, sardines and fruit cocktail. It's something to see, that is.

In Frozen Foods, butterscotch is rippling golden through containers of vanilla ice cream. At the Deli, little squares of cheese slices – each individually wrapped in its own bit of almost invisible plastic – make chequerboards of orange and white in the display case.

The cereals draw me on. They always do. It's the pictures on the boxes. All my flat friends: the Cornflakes Rooster, the Quaker Man with his black hat over all that wool of white hair, Tony the Tiger, and Captain Crunch with all that gold on his blue jacket.

"Nice day today, Sir?" It's the stockboy. I almost don't speak but there is no need to fear here in the Superstore. His eyes say as much.

"Y-Yes," I say. "It's always n-n-nice in the Superstore."

"That's what we like to hear. We wanna keep our customers satisfied."

Around the corner, the candies invite. Hundreds of round twirls of red and peppermint green just spilling over the open bin. There are slabs of white almond bark and dreamy dark chocolate TEMP-TATIONS: today's SPECIAL SAVER at just .48½lb. My mouth is watering and it's only a reach away. The store is still mostly empty. No one is looking. Anything is possible in the Superstore...

Simon says, I dare you: just a taste. My hand is reaching...nearly there in the chocolate dream——no. I stop my hand. Not in the Superstore. It wouldn't be right. Anywhere else maybe. But not in the Superstore.

Just two rows over, the Superstore hostess is in her fresh white smock offering bites of cheese and crackers to the morning shoppers. I take a Diamond Lite from the plate she holds out for me. Her teeth are so white. I'm sure I've seen them before...And then it comes to me: she's the girl on the Pepsident toothpaste box! I'm sure of it! And here she is right in front of me, offering me a bit of cheese on a toothpick. I almost say it...I almost say come to the Superstore with me...But we are here already.

I'm passing the fresh produce – all laid out in special sections lined with wonderfully bright green turf; it's always summer in the Superstore. And there are the peaches like my old tree never knew: rounds of gold and rose with those little hairs that catch the fluorescent light.

There's a long, loud, whirring coming from behind. I turn. The butcher is at the meat counter, grinding bits of beef into soft twists of red. Ham shanks are today's bargain...Compare with the rest, then come back to the best.

I never want to leave. Not ever no way.

I did not mean to go down Aisle 8. I was heading for Aisle 7: cleaning products. But the thought of LYSOL caught in my nostrils and made me turn away. Now I'm in Aisle 8 and there they are. in front of me. One slim gold can after another...NEW FORMULA STAYING POWER SO YOUR HAIR WON'T HAVE STRAYING POWER. It's Pinkie's brand. I'm sure of it.

It's raining today; only splashing but still...Maybe she hasn't remembered to take her umbrella...Oh, oh, oh for the thought of her hair coming undone. Those pretty eyes getting all fearful and twitching again with thoughts of Me and Them. Everything is easy to confuse.

I'm sweating at the thought of her hair coming unstuck. Anti-perspirants: Aisle 6...I know aisle after aisle by heart. I should have known what I would find in Aisle 8. I should have known...

But there is only Pinkie to think of now...How can she feel better than Them if I'm not here to help her feel like Me? What *was* I thinking of when I climbed down down down that dry peach tree. I was not thinking of Pinkie. Forgive me, my nursie-girl.

I eyed the golden cans of FORMULA 17...best not to even think about it. Simon says, take it! I look over either shoulder. Simon *says*! I grab it and run.

I'm running fast but it seems as though everything is running past me faster still; that I'm not running at all...There go the shampoos, the cleansers, the Pepsident Lady and the red twirls of candies...The silver tins are flashing...I'm a blur on the little TV...But will the doors open? I hear the clash of shopping carts. Please let me leave the Superstore. I cannot stay!

The butcher is after me and yelling things. I'm in the parking lot. Just one block, two, to go...My other slipper is flying below that parked chevvy...There's green bottle glass on the pavement green glass in my feet...

He's on me, his great shanks pinning my legs.

The pretty cashier is somewhere behind the last yellow line that I passed. "Don't hurt him, Jim. He's one of the crazies from the Villa."

They bring me back. Pinkie is at Nursie Station B. She smiles like she is meaning, couldn't be helped, and they all shrug their shoulders and smile some more. A nurse is whispering in her ear. Pinkie peeks over the desk and sees the little smear of blood from my feet on the yellow linoleum right in front. She says to go with the nurse. She will bandage my feet.

But I stay and stare at her as always. I have to be sure. I cannot go until I am sure...

Yes, her hair is well stuck to her head.

"Simon?" says the other nursie.

I know her hair will never come unstuck now. I made sure of that today. Even though the butcher got my can of hair spray. I know that her hair will never fly away again.

Pinkie is looking at me like she doesn't know me.

Not at all. She is smiling easily. I am one of Them. It is all clear.

"Well, what does Simon have to say for himself today?"

"N-N-Nothing."

The English Maradona

I've never known an England dressing room like it – after that World Cup one nil defeat by Brazil. Big Alf Addison, one of the two centre backs – he'd played his heart out – after sitting like the rest of us, staring at the floor, got up and hurled his boots against the far wall and then stood, lips tight, chest and shoulders heaving.

Harry Matfen – the cause of the anger – looked up, at Big Alf, the marked wall, the rejected boots, and then at me and grimaced. I turned my head away. Like the others, I wanted to shake and shake him, to ask him why he had done what he had done, especially with only a minute to go and when we were losing. The English Maradona they called him, and even we, his team-mates in the English side, accepted that.

Sam Cartwright, the manager, came in. In his early fifties, fit, no tummy, his face thin and worried. He looked round. "All right. All right. We're still there. We still have a chance. A good one. You didn't deserve to be beat and you thought you hadn't been, that's all."

"That's all," Big Alf repeated bitterly. "Abide by the ref's decisions, you've said. Some of us mustn't have heard you."

"Now, now," Sam raised his hand, palms outwards. "We're not out yet. We have to beat France on Wednesday, and we can do that. And remember, remember," his voice rose and he wagged a finger, "we're here because of *his* individual goals," and he jerked a thumb towards Harry. "You've all said that."

"And we could be out because of him," said Alf.

Sam stood before Harry. Harry glanced up at him. I knew Harry wouldn't explain, wouldn't apologise. We were all quiet, wanting to hear what Sam said.

"You seemed to head that ball, Harry," he said.

Harry shook his head. "Didn't, Sam."

"You could just have thought you handled it, you know."

"I handled it, Sam."

Sam stared at him a long time then said, "Cromwell once said, 'I beseech you in the bowels of Christ, think it possible you may be mistaken.'"

I wondered where on earth he'd got that from.

Harry said, "I'd have had to say to Cromwell, then, that I wasn't mistaken."

Sam gave a great sigh. "All right, even if you did handle it – how about swings and roundabouts?"

"You mean I should have pretended I hadn't?"

Sam snapped, "I'm thinkin' of the times we've scored a good goal and had it disallowed."

"Well, we didn't in this match, Sam, and anyway, I didn't think about it."

"Bloody pity," Alf shouted.

A little later, Harry on his way to the big bath and showers, sat down beside me spreading his towel over his lap.

"Big Alf," he said, "he's in a bit of a state."

"Ya," I said.

"Anyway, he's not moaning about someone at the back this time."

"No, no one at the back," I said.

After a few moments, Harry, testing me, said, "Finish that chess game tonight, Steve?"

"I don't know."

"Why not?"

"I think I'll get drunk."

He fiddled about with his towel, then began to get up, reluctantly. "We can beat France," he said.

"Sure, and they can wallop us. Even if it's a draw, we pack our bags – out, finished."

"We deserved a draw with Brazil," he said. "Didn't you think so?"

"Get your shower, Harry, I said.

He stood up, hurt I knew, but he tried again. "I'm ringing Sandra tonight, Steve."

"Okay; which night don't you ring her."

He turned away and clutching his towel trudged to the showers. A slim, undistinguished-looking figure showing marks at the back of his legs where some swiping tackles had managed to catch him. He evaded most of them. He hated going down. I've never known a striker, except George Best, hit the ground less than Harry Matfen.

But you've hit the ground this time, son, I thought. And you're too dumb to know it. Hitting the ground was a metaphor, of course. Oh, I know the difference between the literal truth and a metaphor. I wrote my own autobiography. Ted Rowland checked it. Ted had to ghost all of Harry's. I knew Ted would be outside in the press room, with the other reporters. I wondered what he'd say, what he'd think, about Harry this time.

Harry and I come from the same town in the North East and we met when we played for the town's boys' team. He was already playing for England Boys, and when I was made substitute for an international we became real friends when we travelled to London together and even though we lived in different parts of the town we would visit each other. He was quiet, a listener. He was naive. He's still naive. We played for the same team after we left school at fifteen, but Harry was first to be an apprentice and first to sign professional for a Football League club. He was in the full England squad at twenty – imagine that. Three years ahead of me. You may have gathered that I'm the stronger personality, and that's true – but it's only off the field.

Something comes over Harry when he puts on a football strip. On the park he holds himself differently, proudly, with authority. His expression changes, his eyes, his lips. He becomes concentrated. He can look at me during a game and snap out a command in a way he would never do off the field. He shouts, he swears, when he's playing. He never does at any other time. I can catch his eye when we're playing, but there'll be no friendly response. Off the field his face will crumple into a smile as soon as I glance at him. The pitch is his domain. He was made for it. The English Maradona. What presence, ability, skills: the flicks, lobs; and he's two-footed, not as dependant on his left as Maradona is. His passing is a dream, short or longish, it's there, in the right place, at the right speed. And brave – too brave, I've thought. And, as I've said, concentrated – when he misses with a shot it's never by much. A perfect player…and to think he could well have put us out of the World Cup.

I've had to work far harder at things, and life has worried me off the field, especially women. There've been times when I've found it difficult to concentrate. Not so Harry. Sandra went to the same school, lived two doors away, they were going about with each other when they were sixteen and were married at twenty. I'd say he was more in love with her now, if that is possible. She's part of him.

His being with Sandra from so early on spoiled our friendship when we were lads. He was never really one of the lads because of that. We got close again when I joined United, where he was, and more so when I married.

And there's the money side. He's never worried about it. *I've* been more concerned on his behalf and even spoke up for him at United, which did my standing no good, and then I got him a good agent. I know far more about the money and contract side than Harry. I always seem to be in dispute over contracts. Harry's never in dispute – of course clubs and sponsors want him more than they want me.

So he's been settled all his life – without money, love or sex problems. And he's not frightened to talk of his mother – she had most to do with the sort of chap he is. I remember when we were boys going across to see him during a school holiday. He was out doing some shopping for her and when he came in – before she would let him out to play football – she checked the groceries he'd got and found he'd been given a pound of margerine instead of half a pound which he'd asked for and paid for. She told him to take the extra half pound back straight away, which he did. I went with him, fuming at the delay in our playing. But Harry wasn't upset. He said he ought to have seen the mistake himself at the time and handed them back the half pound.

Harry's always been ahead of me. But, I thought in that miserable dressing room, that what he'd done in the Brazil game could be the turning point. That he could drop behind now, especially if we didn't beat France on Wednesday, and frankly I don't think we will.

What happened was this: with Brazil leading by the only goal, with one minute left, I just managed to lob a ball into the box for Harry to have a go at with his head. As it left me I felt it was going to be a shade too high, but as their goalie rushed out to punch away, Harry rose, head and balancing hand clear, and then headed the ball past the keeper and into the net for an equaliser.

We raced to him, swarmed round him, fell on him, hugged him, but Harry, after a moment or two, began wrenching himself free, gasping, "No, no." He thrust us aside, ran away from us, past the despondent Brazilian defenders and towards the referee who, after signalling a goal, was making for the centre spot. And when he got to him Harry began talking, gesticulating. He held up his hand and hit the back of it. Fearing what he was saying I raced down, and I was right: Harry was telling the referee that he hadn't headed the ball in, it had hit the back of his hand and gone in.

I tried to drag him away. I shouted at the referee, "Don't listen, ref. He doesn't know what he's saying. It was a good goal. You saw it. They're not protesting. He's round the bend." The ref ordered me away, sternly, and arms crossed listened intently to Harry. Not understanding all the words, no doubt, but getting the meaning. Then – it was unbelievable – he changed his decision. He disallowed the goal and gave Brazil a free kick in their box for hands against Harry. The lads, amazed, distraught, protested, but the referee waved them off. They turned then on Harry, but the Brazilians took their free kick quickly – in case the referee changed his mind again, and we had to get busy to stop them scoring a second.

I've seen such behaviour as Harry's in innocent schoolboy football but never in the professional game and here it was at a vital moment in a World Cup game. I thought it stupid, self-indulgent; that Harry had not thought of his team-mates and manager and of all the millions back home in England wanting us to succeed. And surely it is a matter of swings and roundabouts, as Sam said.

In the dressing room, Harry, ready to leave, came and stood beside me as I put my tie on. "The press are after me," he said.

And the television and radio," I added.

He wasn't good at interviews.

As I pictured him before them, squirming, making halting, inadequate replies, I felt compassion. "See a steward – there may be a way out at the back or the side," I said.

He stood. "Fancy old Sam coming out with that Cromwell stuff," he said.

"Aye, people are funny," I said.

"Well, I'll face them," he said slowly.

"Okay. See you," I said and walked past him. Outside Ted Rowland was standing against the wall, examining his notebook. He smiled wanly. He knew I would speak to him alone. I said to him, "Harry'll never live this down, Ted. Did you ever see the like of it – and in such a match, at such a time. You'd think he was playing for a goody goody boys club."

"Or the old Corinthians," Ted said.

"We could be out of the World Cup because of it," I said.

"We probably are," he said, and then he surprised me, by adding, "Not that it will do Harry any harm."

"Of course it will," I snapped. "Harry could be on the downgrade after today. He's not reliable. Not professional. You should have been in that dressing room."

Ted heaved himself clear of the wall and motioned me further away from the others. "Harry's star's not falling," he said, "and Sam would be finished if he dropped him. Drop him for being honest: Sam would be crucified. Can't you see that what Harry did was greater than scoring a goal. In comparison goals are two a penny. To admit, plead, that you haven't scored, when everyone, but everyone, thought you had – wonderful."

I shook my head and muttered, "You've got it wrong."

Ted went on, "The people back home will love it. The world will love it. Every country will wish it was one of their men who'd done it. But it was an Englishman. Oh, oh, the English Maradona does not cheat." He gripped my shoulder and leant forward nearly speaking in my ear. "Steve, people will tell of it with tears of pride in their eyes. And it's all on tape, the whole thing. BBC and ITV. Ready to be shown again and again over the years – a moving picture of honest, magnaminous, sporting behaviour. An example to the world. Steve, Harry became a legend today."

"No," I said, without conviction.

"Yes, and, I wouldn't be surprised if he made the birthday honours list – funnier things have happened."

I stared at him.

"You thought he was made before," he said, "You ain't seen nothing yet. Wait till you see the editorials. Diego Maradona will now have to try to be the Argentine Harry Matfen."

I played chess with Harry that night after all.

A Cold Morning

Philip was cold when he woke up. His hand groped for the jacket which he had laid across his knees the night before; they had taken a blanket for the baby, leaving him feeling chilly under his covers.

Climbing from the mattress he scuttled his stiff limbs into the clothes which lay as he'd left them on the floor; school flannel trousers, jersey, socks. Still shivering he put the jacket on as well.

He was feeling hungry. What time was it? His mam would start shouting if he if he made a noise downstairs too early. The sky through the window looked dark and he couldn't make out the hands of the church clock. It was raining. In the street below a woman with an umbrella hurried on her way to work; it must be morning.

On the landing he put an ear to their door. Would they be awake? His mother was sleeping in there with the new man called Raymond she'd brought home last night. He was nice so far, had told him jokes and given him money for fish and chips, but Philip knew better than to like him too soon. Men in the house meant trouble; always there were arguments which sent him out into the street to escape. Playing with his mates was good but after dark there seemed nowhere to go.

He could hear nothing. Pressing his ear to the door he listened for the sound of the bed creaking; still nothing. Carefully he eased it open to look inside.

"Mam…"

There was nobody. On the floor lay the usual litter of beer cans and cigarette ash but the bed was empty. Maybe Raymond hadn't stayed after all; his mam might be feeding the baby downstairs. He crept down the lino stairs, curling his toes at the cold creeping into his socks.

"Mam?"

She wasn't in the living room either. Only the baby lay sleeping on the settee covered by a grey blanket, her hand curled against her cheek; she was making sucking noises. Soon she would wake and want food; maybe his mother was in the kitchen preparing her bottle. But there was no noise of a tap running, no noise at all.

By the sink stood the unrinsed bottle with the rubber teat still in place. On the table lay the remains of food they'd brought in last night; foil containers smelling of curry, an end of bread, a tub of margerine. Sugar had spilled from its packet on to the floor; since his mother wasn't there to stop him he scooped some into his palm, licking it with his tongue. He couldn't find the knife so he tore at the loaf and dipped pieces into the margerine. At the sink he washed a dirty cup for a drink of water.

The noise of the tap woke the baby who began wailing from under her blanket. For a while he continued to eat but as the cries grew he knelt on the floorboards beside her; "Samantha, Sammy, Sammy, Sammy! Mam's coming soon."

Now that she could see him the baby stopped crying and began to coo and smile. Probably mam had gone out to the shop for milk, though it wasn't like her to be up so early. His mother didn't go to work so she lay in bed late in the mornings. If there was no milk or bread he ran to the store before school. She didn't like being woken up for money so he never asked, just took it from her purse on the table or persuaded Mr. Patel to write it in the book on his counter. In the right mood he could be talked into parting with a bottle of milk or a loaf, though never sweets. Philip had tried but always the shopkeeper said no.

"Each day your mother buys sweets for you, too many sweets. Am I to give you more?"

He looked for the purse but it was not in its usual place on the table. She must be at the shop around the corner, and she would be back soon. Samantha would have to wait.

As if she guessed his thoughts the baby once more began crying and this time would not be comforted. He scooped her up in a blanket and walked with her for a while but she was awkward to hold; his arms ached. When he laid her down again on the cold cushion she was furious and screamed until her face was red and crumpled. If only his mam would come back with the milk.

The crying grew worse. He knew she needed food, but the only milk in the kitchen was a stale inch at the bottom of last night's feeding bottle. Fetching this he stuck the teat in her mouth;

"Sup sups Samantha! Mammy's bringing some more soon."

The baby's tongue thrust the cold teat from her and she began to splutter. Milk dribbled across her face; he watched a damp patch grow as her vest absorbed it. Probably her nappy was wet as well; sometimes she screamed to be changed. He'd try that.

Leaving her to cry he looked about for a clean nappy. The wash bucket in the kitchen was full; the smell took his breath as he searched through the mound of clothes around it. Hanging from a chair was half an old towel which he had seen his mother use when she was behind with the wash; it would do for now.

He was used to the routine of cleaning and changing his sister but this morning's screams and kicks made the job harder.

"Mam's coming with the milkies soon," he soothed, but her cries continued until, just as he was about to fasten the pin they stopped. This frightened him. He peered into her face and was thankful to see her mouth trying to feed from the fist she'd stuffed into it.

The church clock began to strike as he was wrapping the blanket around her, seven, eight, nine. Time to go to school, he was late already, but what to do about the baby? He thought of leaving her on the settee; maybe his mother wouldn't be too long with the milk. Then she began to cry again; he saw disappointment and temper spread across her face as she discovered the emptiness of her own hand.

To stop the cries he lifted her again, carrying her round the room as he searched for his shoes among the muddle of things. Stuffing his feet into them he reached with one hand for the doorknob and stepped out into the rain, taking Samantha with him.

His mother wasn't in Patel's shop. As he peered through the steamy window a man came out carrying a paper. Seeing the baby in his arms he hesitated, seemed about to speak but walked away. Philip continued in the direction of school which was a block further on, beyond the church.

He could see Miss Rose through the window with her glasses on, marking the register already. Clasping his sister to him he struggled across the playground to the classroom door which he kicked open with his foot.

"Philip!" the teacher seemed alarmed to see him in the doorway with his bundle.

"I'm sorry I'm late, Miss but I had to bring the baby." Miss Rose closed the door to shut out the cold and urged him towards the stove, taking the baby from him. He could see shock on her face as she touched Samantha's hands and feet.

"She's cold. I'll fetch the medical blanket and we'll make a bed for her."

"And she needs feeding," said Philip. "Our milk was all used up this morning."

With Samantha settled in a tidy box and Miss Rose in control Philip felt better. He stuck his feet nearer to the warmth and watched steam rise from his shoes. There was a row of apples on the shelf behind her desk; most mornings she let them stand by the stove before lessons to eat fruit or biscuits and talk; she'd be sharing them soon.

But instead she asked the class to sit at their desks and gave out workbooks, telling them to find today's page.

"I explained this work to you yesterday. I'd like you to fill in the answers while I'm out of the room. All of you are to stay in place and make no noise; remember we have a baby with us."

In her absence the class began whispering, asking him "What did you bring the baby for?"

"I had to," he told them. "My mam had gone out."

Miss Rose was gone for a long time. Some children sneaked out of their places to peep at the sleeping baby. The girls were saying how lovely she was with ooohs and ahhhs and making baby noises. Philip felt proud.

"Don't wake her," he warned; "She's not been fed yet."

When the teacher came back she shooed them to their seats but kept Philip beside her, asking him questions in a low voice so that the rest of the class couldn't hear;

"Why did you need to bring the baby to school? Were you left alone? Has this happened before?"

She was looking closely at him. In her dark eyes he saw tiny reflections of himself. He noticed for the first time darkish hair on her upper lip, a moustache, almost.

"Well?"

He didn't know what to tell her. Although he liked Miss Rose he knew from his mother not to talk too much about their home. A social worker called Ted sometimes visited the house to drink a cup of tea and talk. His mam always sent him out to play when he came. When she went out in the evenings she warned him to let nobody into the house.

"When I'm out, don't answer. Like as not it'll be somebody come to take you away."

Some nights when she'd gone he lay awake in the dark for ages, listening for a knock on the door.

"I'm waiting."

Miss Rose always said this when she was going to get annoyed. He could hear her breathing, slowly in then out, still staring at him. He'd have to make up something.

"My mam's gone to town. For some food for Samantha. She's hungry now; can I go for some milk? Just to keep her going till my mam gets back?"

This only led to more questions about what time his mother set out, was she there when he woke up, was he alone.

He didn't mean to bring Raymond into his answers but a mention of "they" brought on so many questions that he found himself saying

"He's not as bad as the others. He bought me fish and chips."

He was sent to his place then, where he sat looking with longing at the apples warming on the shelf. She was a long time handing them out today. Thoughts of the baby must have put it out of her mind. Maybe he should have left Samantha at home after all and come to school on his own like other mornings. His coat was damp, his feet were cold and he could not read the words lined up on the page in front of him. Yesterday he'd been praised for knowing these same answers.

The morning seemed very long. At break Miss Rose dismissed the class.

"The rain has stopped but I don't want any of you running through puddles. Some people's feet have only just dried out from this morning."

He stood up to leave with the rest but she kept him back, giving him a story book to read. When he asked to go to the toilet she waited outside the door until he came out, then walked beside him into the classroom. He felt embarassed and wished she would stop watching him.

After a while Miss Tattersall, the Headmistress came in with a bottle bought from the chemist and a tin of expensive baby food.

"Is this what she usually has?"

He agreed that it was although his mam normally fed Samantha on ordinary milk. She would have called the special food expensive rubbish but he wasn't going to risk more questions by telling them that. The two women fussed over his baby and tried to get her to take the milk. She started to cry and sounded hungry but she wouldn't suck from the new bottle. Watching their awkward efforts Philip wished they'd let him feed her, or better still, take her home. Surely his mam would be there by now.

After break it was maths. He tried to make sense of the sums on the card but he couldn't remember how to do them. He put down his pencil and watched Samantha sleeping again in her makeshift bed. She must be hungry after a morning without milk. Soon it would be lunchtime. He would skip the school dinner and ask Miss Rose if he could take his sister home. Maybe he could even persuade her to save a meal for him. It was sausages today, his favourite.

Shortly before twelve the classroom door opened. Miss Tattersall led two strangers inside, a woman with long hair tied with a scarf and an important looking man with a briefcase. She introduced them to Miss Rose who seemed to expect them. Visitors, thought Philip. They'd be coming round the room soon, looking at books; he picked up his pencil to start work.

But instead of walking along the rows the woman went across to the stove and very gently picked up Samantha. Her companion had put down his briefcase and was following Miss Rose down the aisle. They were coming towards him.

"This is Philip."

She was smiling as she reached for his hand.

"Mr Garnett is going to look after you for a while, until your mother comes back."

His stomach heaved. Had something happened to his mam? Was she dead, or lying in a hospital somewhere, unable to reach him?

Then, as he was letting them lead him out it hit him. This was the knock on the door, the man his mother had warned him of. He struggled to pull away but Mr. Garnett had him in a tight grip. His body twisted towards Miss Rose in an appeal for help.

"Here," she said, lifting an apple from the shelf. "Take this with you."

The Wedding

The day dawned wet and the bickering started early. Janice was all for donning her bridesmaid's dress without bothering with a wash. When Mam told her she couldn't wear it till after the hairdresser's she worked herself into a tantrum. In the end Dad had to threaten her with a good hiding if she didn't shut up, and then Mam set on to Dad for threatening her. Jacky came downstairs already wearing his new wedding gear but still moaning about not having a Beatle-style jacket without the lapels that absolutely everybody who was 'with it' was wearing – except him. It set Janice off whining again.

With most of the bathroom queue distracted, it gave me chance to slip in out of turn, so Dad settled for a wash and shave at the kitchen sink while Mam started on the breakfast.

I was inspecting my face for blackheads in the bathroom mirror and speculating how cousin Vera must feel with skin like an arrangement of erupting volcanoes and craters, when the smell of frying bacon percolated upstairs interrupting my meditation.

"I don't want anything to eat," I said, thinking of the fit of the blue satin dress I would be slipping into in a few hours time.

Mam passed over a bacon sandwich. "Get this inside you. There mightn't be time for much dinner and we don't want you falling about all over the place."

"Mam!" I said with exaggerated exasperation. She was referring to my tendency to faint at the slightest provocation since my periods started the previous year. I was secretly proud of my budding womanhood and was eagerly awaiting some indication that my flat chest was going to sprout bosoms. All the same, I was easily embarassed by conversation on the subject.

Don and Jacky sniggered and Mam glared at them. "Get on with your breakfast and don't go spilling anything down you. You shouldn't have put your suit on yet." Jacky surreptitiously wiped the front of his shirt, but not before Mam had seen. "I knew it. You're not fit to have decent clothes. Get that shirt off!" Jacky finished his breakfast in his vest, with a glowing ear where Mam had backhanded him and a stupid smirk on his face.

I was in the bathroom titivating myself when Don kicked the door open. "Soddin'ell, you gunna be in there all day."

He shoved me away from the mirror so I backed out giving him my most contemptuous look and retreated to the bedroom. I caught

Janice rooting through one of my drawers and she jumped guiltily but I pretended not to notice. "That Don is disgusting! Do you know what he's just said to me?" She was all ears. "I'd better not say though, you're too young."

"Did he swear at you?" she demanded eagerly.

"He certainly did," I sneered disdainfully. I'd been practising that disdainful sneer all week and this was my first real opportunity to use it. It had the desired effect.

She bounded off the bed and out of the door like a shot. "Dad, Dad," she yelled. "Our Don's been swearing again!"

Don emerged from the bathroom and grabbed her. "Shut up you little snot." He twisted her arm and she yelled.

"You leave that girl alone and I won't have you swearing in this house." Dad's voice came up the stairs.

Don gave Janice's arm another twist, she gave another yell and Dad's tread could be heard on the stairs. Then there was a lot of yelling and shouting on the landing and Mam came up to sort it out. I kept out of it but I was quite satisfied with my bit of manipulation!

We were due at the hairdresser's at 10 o'clock and would have been there on time if it hadn't been for the shirt. I was in a dither in case we got sent home again uncoiffured, for being late. Going to the hairdresser was a real experience. It was the first time I'd ever been to a proper hairdresser. Mam always cut our hair and what we lacked in style was compensated by economy and easy maintenance. She'd acquired her hairdressing skills under the tuition of Aunty Mavis, who'd done 6 weeks as an apprentice hairdresser with Leslie Francis before her hands had broken out in huge, red, weeping sores. Severe allergies to essential chemicals cut short her career but she felt she'd learned enough in that time to apply her skills to the rest of the family, though I doubt Leslie Francis would have agreed with her assessment. She trained my Mam in the basics in exchange for being taught how to turn sock heels. But for all that Mam's hairdressing skills were sufficient for everyday wear, she didn't consider them adequate for this occasion.

By the time we got to the hairdresser's the Blacklidge contingent were already underway. Sheila and Aunty Amy were already under 2 of the 3 dryers, Grandma Bailey was about to go under, Sheila'a Grandma Blacklidge was being rollered and Aunty Doris with wet crinkly hair dripping onto a stained towel was waiting her turn. All except Vera, she was made to wait because bridesmaids took priority, but she was engrossed in a dated copy of Valentine, no doubt the only romance that ever entered her barren world.

Vera was almost the same age as me but wasn't to be a bridesmaid. Ostensibly because she lived in Blackburn, and it wasn't considered practical to organise wedding plans and a bridesmaid dress at long distance, but I suspect the real reason was because she had prominent teeth and periodic but severe bouts of acne. There was the unspoken fear that the excitement might trigger an outbreak of acne just before the wedding and spoil the big day, not to mention the photographs.

As soon as she saw us Aunty Amy emerged from under her plastic dome. It was difficult to tell whether her tight faced expression was because we were late or because of the assortment of tightly wound, pink and green, jumbo, spikey, plastic hair rollers that made the skin of her forehead wrinkle-free and shiny, and gave her a slighty oriental cast.

"What kept you?" She flicked her head at the Blackburn Blacklidges to indicate they'd gone out of turn because of us. "You know what it's like with the kids..." said Mam. Aunty Amy didn't, Sheila was her only child. Thin-lipped she resubmerged under her transparent hive.

I waited my turn clutching a picture of Jean Shrimpton, then showed it to Doreen's shampoo girl. Taking my place at the backwash sink, I put myself completely in her hands and confidently expected to emerge fully transformed – six inches taller, half a stone slimmer and ravishing.

Two hours later; shampooed and trimmed, rollered and dried, tightly backcombed and elaborately curled, well pinned and stiffly laquered, with faces of lobster hue, we all trooped out – not the slightest resemblance to Jean Shrimpton among us. What we did resemble however, as the photographs later testified – with huge grotesque heads precariously balanced on stiffly held necks, was a gathering of squat, deformed dwarfs.

But at the time we felt like the bees' knees. So preening and cavorting, the nine of us stopped off at the fish and chip shop on the way back to Aunty Amy's. We were admired by the queue, flaunted details of the wedding to those not already in the know, and ordered fish, chips and mushy peas for seventeen, courtesy of Aunty Amy. The revels had officially begun.

I balanced on a settee arm eating carefully so as not to disturb my hairdo. Though with tresses as rigid as chicken wire and concrete, the arrangement should be good for a week at least. I devoured my dinner still mindful of the possible effect of two recent meals on the fit of my bridesmaid dress. Mam ranted at Jacky as she worked on the pea-green stain on the front of his red tie

The flowers were delivered and buttonholes given to the favoured few. Away relatives were allocated to the bathroom facilities of home based relatives and were dispersed around the neighbourhood to change into their wedding finery. We waited for the chaos to diffuse as the number of bodies reduced and then the female protagonists in the bridal party went upstairs to start getting ready.

After removing the fish and chip grease, me and Janice shared Sheila's bedroom. I dabbled in her make-up and under her guidance settled for a layer of Pan-Stick, a touch of pale blue eye-shadow to complement my dress and a smothering of mascara — which gave my mortifyingly small, deepset eyes a Dusty Springfield look. Janice was allowed a touch of powder and pale lipstick to stop her whining. Sheila, who'd read in some beauty magazine that a dusting of green powder would tone down the redness of a flushed skin, applied a liberal dose of green powder eyeshadow to her cheeks and nose. Her colour was very high, from excitement, the effect of the hairdryer or a bit of both — but her face glowed. Beads of sweat popped out on her forehead like a tiara to complement the borrowed rhinestone necklace. She became more and more frantic as the green eyeshadow, instead of toning down her redness, gave her an unearthly phosphorescent gleam, in an extra-terrestrial sort of a way.

Aunty Amy came into the bedroom in a cerise dress and jacket and a matching petalled hat. It put me in mind of a large pink peony balanced on her head. She'd come to oversee the donning of the wedding dress and the veil, a task I understood to be the chief bridesmaid's job and I was a bit peeved at not being considered up to the responsibility. She didn't help Sheila's distress by asking if she felt bilious. (Aunty Amy always acted like they were posher than us — we were sick and had the trots, they had biliousness and diarrhoea.) Sheila burst into tears and Aunt Amy bustled her into the bathroom to apply cold water to her face.

Meanwhile, I helped Janice to dress and then I fussed and fiddled with layers of net underskirts. Slowly and carefully I stretched the tan stockings over my legs and attached them to the rubber buttons of my new suspender belt. After inspecting my legs I admired my bosoms in my first bra; 30AA cup and covered with little pink rose buds. I polished specks of dust off my new white shoes and then I fastened the white satin flowers in my hair. And all the time everybody was on at me to hurry up. But I was not to be rushed.

The vision I was savouring was not to be shared — not straight away. I waited till I was alone. Standing in front of the full length mirror, I closed my eyes and mindful of my hair, carefully slipped the satin dress over my head. I patted the sides of my head in case a hair had come adrift and opened my eyes.

What did I expect to see? A rhapsody in blue, a blue moon, a moody blue? What I saw was a reflection of myself with a large ornamental head in a pretty blue frock, except the hem dipped a little at the side. Mildly disappointed with the image, I tugged at the skirt and it levelled up till I moved so I hitched it up from the waist. I adopted a more relaxed stance and with my hip stuck out and my weight on my left leg, the hem looked level. I bore that in mind for when I was in the public eye. The red patch on my chin still lingered where I'd recently squeezed another blackhead so I applied another dab of Pan-Stick. Life could be so cruel. Jean Shrimpton had little to worry about but perhaps Rita Tushingham ought to watch out.

Sheila emerged from the bathroom. Cold water cancelled the green look, the redness and the tears. Sheila reapplied her make-up and when she was satisfied, climbed into the wonderful candyfloss confection of skirts and lace and frills and bows and embroidered roses. Aunt Amy and Mam stood back to admire. Their oooohs and ahhhhs, deep sighs and beaming smiles said it all. Enough to change Sheila's watery smile into a real grin. Her dress and hair and veil and shining eyes and lovely smile were really beautiful and I would have cried if it hadn't been for my mascara. She'd have looked just like a real fairy princess if she hadn't been so fat.

When the car arrived to convey bridesmaids and bride's mother to the church, Mam came too. I sat next to the window so the people standing at the kerb could see me. I bestowed them with my regal smile and a small wave which produced a silly giggle from Janice and a "just who do you think you are now" sigh from Mam, so I concentrated on looking aloof and unapproachable. The journey to the church was over in moments: it was only at the bottom of the street. Plenty of people were standing outside the church door and others drifted out of the Cross Keys, summoned by the arrival of our car.

Malc standing with his best man, looked like a condemned man smoking his last cigarette. He gazed at the crowd as if he were no part of it. Twitching at his tie, smoothing his pockets – ready to brazen it through or ready to run? The choice was taken from him as we climbed out of the car. It was a signal for the stragglers to take their places. Malc nodded at us, doffed his cig and entered the church. Don and Jacky as sidesmen, allocated ours and theirs to the correct side.

The sky was still more grey than blue and a biting wind made the clouds scud across. We stood in the shelter of the door arch to await the bride. Once they'd established their places Mam and Aunty Amy came out again to wait with us. We waited. Tired of waiting I went inside to inspect the congregation from the back of the church. It was a good turn out, more of our side than there were of Malc's, but weddings and funerals alike, you could always count on our lot to swell the numbers.

Organ music played quietly. I ventured further inside to see who I could identify, I went almost as far as the centre aisle. Bored with waiting Jacky took a swing at me with his foot, trying to trip me up. I dodged it and his foot clunked hollowly against a pew. Thinking the action was about to start people turned for an early glimpse of the bride. Dad caught my eye and waved, I waved back, The vicar stretched his neck and came up the aisle towards us. Red faced, Jacky gave an apologetic wave and the vicar raised his hand in acknowledgement and unfortunately the organist took it as a signal.

The music abruptly changed to the wedding march. Mam and Aunty Amy started into the church looking puzzled, as if suspecting that Sheila and Uncle Bill had somehow given them the slip. Mam pointed her finger at Jacky. She didn't need to say anything, we were well familiar with the gesture. I dashed past her, back to the door, leaving Jacky to take the rap. Realizing his mistake the organist switched tunes again. Mam was just coming to start on me when Sheila's car drew up.

"She's here," yelled Janice loud enough for everyone to hear and the organist took up the wedding march again.

Squeezing through the car door with voluminous bunches of lace and net skirts in her arms, Sheila tried not to crush her dress. We dashed to her and disaster struck. Catching her stiletto heel in her train, the net tangled round her shoe. Unaware, she took a couple of steps and yanked veil and headdress off her head. Hair and hair-pins came with it. Mam and Aunty Amy rushed to the rescue of the headdress while me and Uncle Bill tried to disentangle her heel. Sheila, hopping on one leg with her head down, stumbled, landed on one knee and rolled over onto a well cushioned thigh. Janice tried to save the bouquet from being crushed and a clump of freesias and stephanotis came off in her hand. Sheila's face resumed its former redness, tears welled and held for a moment, then slid down her face forming rivulets on her powdered cheeks. The organist played the wedding march for the third time.

Aunt Amy set about repositioning the tiara, and with hanky and spit, repaired the ravaged make-up as best she could. Mam, who never went anywhere without a needle and cotton, did a repair job on the train. I shoved the flowers back into the bouquet and hoped they'd at least survive the service, Sheila snivelled, Uncle Bill stood around looking uselesss and Janice took it upon herself to relay details of the disaster to those at the back of the church. When the organist switched to Lead Kindly Light we knew the news had filtered through to the front. The vicar came out to investigate the delay and was soon followed by restless guests nipping out for cigarettes, shortly joined by early arrivals for the wedding coming after.

It took a while to patch Sheila up, recompose her and reorganise the guests, but given the signal, the organist had another shot at the wedding march and the bridal party trooped down the aisle as if on cue.

We covered the length of the aisle without a hitch, apart from one of the freezias dropping out when Sheila handed me her bouquet. I don't think she noticed though and I poked it with my toe till it dropped down the narrow, fancy iron grid in the flagged stone floor. Nevertheless, when it came to the "Who giveth this woman..." Uncle Bill handed her over with unseemly eagerness, to my way of thinking.

I tried to absorb the words of the ceremony but my thoughts distracted me. I wanted to be swept up in the beauty and romance of the occasion; but though Malc wasn't bad looking and was quite a snappy dresser, there was a certain something about him that didn't fit any of my romantic hero images. Perhaps it was his roughness? His hands carried the blue scars of mining injuries and the blackheads on the back of his neck matched the grime under his chewed finger-nails. Even with Beatle haircut and suit his coarse features lacked the sensitivity of an eloquent soul.

Malc kneeled at the altar. Sheila struggled to lower herself grace-fully, descended the last few inches in a rush and saved herself from falling forwards by grabbing the vicar's legs. Her skirt trapped and stretched taught under ample knees, she shuffled and struggled to straighten up, putting considerable stress on the fabric of the dress. Two pearl buttons popped off the back fastening, the material gaped, revealing a few inches of pink, dimpled flesh. One button bounced and disappeared down the fancy iron grid and the other rolled a surprising distance and came to rest at the base of the pulpit. A choirboy sniggered. And Sheila, probably feeling a draught tried to grope discreetly behind her back and close the gap.

"Please God, don't make me laugh," I prayed desperately. My eyes inspected the vaulted ceiling, studiously gazed at the stained glass windows, travelled the length of the front pews noting the variey of wedding hats and eventually came to rest on my new white shoes. I was entranced by the perfection of my white feet clad in real pointy winklepickers, and with two inch high stiletto heels and metal tips that click-clacked satisfyingly whenever I walked.

I concentrated on them intently until the uncontrollable urge to giggle passed. Then believing myself mistress of my emotions I raised my eyes a little till they settled on the soles of Malc's brand new brown shoes. Across the left sole was a red and white sale ticket, the writing still clearly legible. "£9/19/11 reduced to £7/19/11." A second label partially overstuck the first and proclaimed – "Special bargain – £2/19/11 – odd sizes." In the centre of the left instep it said 8, in the middle of the right instep it said 10.

I took a sharp breath. I coughed and tried to suppress it. My throat closed up. I gasped and choked and gasped again. I felt my face go red with the effort. I bent over and coughed and strained to clear my air passages and my stomach heaved in sympathy. Then the unthinkable happened. I clasped my hand over my mouth but there was no holding it back. Half digested fish, chips and mushy peas spewed forth. It covered my hand, splattered the front of my dress and settled in a heap in the middle of Sheila's lace train.

Covered in vomit, saliva and humiliation I crouched and tried to scoop up the disgusting mess. I looked around for somewhere to secrete it. The ornate iron grid came to mind but before I had chance to dispose of it I recognised the feet standing before me. My mother's new shoes. She took my arm. "C'mon, let's get you cleaned up," she sighed. Shamefaced I stood up, still clutching my burden. I held out two full hands to her, as if in supplication. She shook her head and moved towards the vestry. I followed with lowered eyes, keeping sufficient distance between us to protect her new suit from my contamination. I could hear Sheila's wailing voice as I was led away. There was a bit of a commotion and then the vicar took control and carried on with the wedding – we were running nearly an hour late and other brides were apparently queueing at the door.

The rest of the day passed as an anti-climax. I considered it more advantageous to play up vague symptoms of my affliction to stave off reprisals. I perhaps overplayed. Mam and Aunty Amy in particular thought it better if I didn't eat much, especially anything too rich – so at the wedding feast I just ended up with a bit of lettuce and a slice of boiled ham – no trifle, no buns, not even any wedding cake! Probably spite on Aunty Amy's part and I was sent home early because she said I looked flushed – just as the evening revels were starting and the local band was warming up in the church hall.

It was months before Sheila spoke to me again. Aunt Amy was less forgiving. And it was years before I could recall the details of that wedding without cringing at the memory of my humiliation.

Sheila was in the middle of a protracted and acrimonious divorce. We went out for a drink to help take her mind off it. When she started reminiscing on her miserable marriage and miserly husband, I reminded her of her wedding day farce and filled her in on some of the details she'd missed at the time. That's the trouble with gin – it makes me giggle uncontrollably or maudlingly sentimental. This time it was both.

"If only you'd said about his shoes at the time." Gloomily she knocked back another drink. "If I'd had your insight on his penny-pinching soul, perhaps I wouldn't have married the tight-fisted bastard in the first place."

David Almond

Nesting

For years he'd pestered her with, *Tell me what it was like when I was in you. Tell me what it was like before I was here.*

For years she'd told him. But as he grew older, he began never to ask. And she began only on bright mornings ever to tell.

☆

It was spring. The streetlights were on. Blackbirds had stopped singing in the hedges.

"Stay inside," she said, "just one night."

He perched on the edge of his chair, with his jacket on his knee.

"Stephen!"

It was her pleading voice, the one he hated.

"Just goin f'ra while," he muttered. "Not long."

"You'd protect me, Stephen. Soon as he went you said you would. Now I'll be the man, you said. The man."

"An' I will. Tellin y'I will."

"Tellin's nothin. Stay inside."

He crouched and fiddled with his shoelaces, fastening them viciously tight.

"They come through the windows, Stephen, even when you're in. Doesn't matter if you're in. They wait in the gardens for the men to leave. They come in quiet wi'their knives and snooker cues, wi'stockins on their faces. *Woman keep still,* they tell you. *Not a move or you'll get what's comin. Where is it?* they ask. Stephen, what'll I tell them when there's nowt?"

"So what's to come for if there's nowt?"

"That's it. What they left with? Me. Nowt but me. Stephen, stay inside."

"There's nobody, woman. Who'd want to get in here?"

He followed the street's long curve, turned into the narrow alley that led him out through the fringes onto the waste. Out there the ground dropped, a sudden quickening of the miles-long slope towards the sea. Once there'd been a few streets here, almost a village. There were a few stone remnants blanketed by bramble and ivy, thin strips of garden still marked by rampant hedges. Spreading out from it was a circle of paltry spoilheaps, and deep gashes in the earth that had become the estate's dumps. Years ago, with the other kids, he'd spend whole days roaming the hillside, searching the hedges for nests. The ruined streets had been their ghost town, where they'd play until the long scary shadows came and sent them running, filled with laughter and fright, back toward the brand new houses.

Now the other kids went other ways. They took buses into the city that was already burning the sky beyond the crest. They gathered in the estate's community centres and clubs. And, it was true, there were those who did prowl the curving streets, poised to take their chances.

He shuddered and went down, taking a narrow cindered track, ancient waggonway edged with dense hawthorn hedges. He knew it all, even in the dark. After a quarter mile or so, he turned right, ducking through towards a cottage less dilapidated than most. It smelt of shit in there, and massive thistles grew out through the floor. But there were walls almost as tall as he was, with strips of bleached paper still attached behind the creepers. A single window frame remained, a square filled with the slope, the silhouettes of factories at the top, the burning sky. He lowered himself onto the collection of cushions and rags he'd months ago dragged from the dumps. He emptied his pockets: an aerosol, a plastic bag. He sprayed the aerosol until there was a pool in the corner of the bag. He wrapped the bag around his face and breathed deeply. He went on breathing, tightening the bag's opening against his cheeks, pushing his lips closer and closer, waiting for the darkness to deepen, for the thundering of blood to begin.

The day he left, she had Stephen singing. They sat together on the sofa, looking out into the street. Her voice started it:

Clap hands for Daddy coming
Down the waggonway
His pockets full of money
And his hands all clay...

She kept leaving him, scanning from the window, returning to him. She smiled. "Come on, Stephen. What's wrong? Too big to sing now?" She took his hands, clapped them between her own.

Clap hands for Daddy coming
Down the waggonway...

They went on waiting as far as dusk and beyond. He lay against her breast and felt her trembling. "Sing," she whispered. "Sing."

He sang. He was twelve years old then. He'd been born here, when the estate was a riddle of foundation trenches, half-made roads, half-formed walls. His infancy had been accompanied by the clink of trowels, the suck and smack of piledrivers, the bulleting of pneumatic drills. On expeditions out, strapped into the Silver Cross that lurched on rubble and underfill, he stared out from beneath the dark hood to watch his mother cursing, grinning through her sweat, singing at him, calling to the foremen, "Will it ever all be done?" She taught him the ring of streets, the alleyways out onto the slope, the wilderness outside, the distant sea. She showed him the factories being massively assembled around the crest. "That's where Daddy'll go," she told him. "When it's all done, he'll be in there, workin the machines." As he grew older, between the men going up in the morning and their coming back at night, he learned the dusty silence of the streets, the afternoons disturbed only by children playing, mothers calling, the endless droning from the crest. "And's how it ought to be," his father would say. "Whole places made for them like us. Homes put here, work put here. So's it's all clean and new and settled fr'a change, and you feel you're worth somethin wi' a life worth lookin forward to. Right, lass? Bloody aye." Sundays he'd take Stephen out, leaving the Silver Cross to gleam uselessly in the kitchen. "Mother's stuff," he'd say. "The lad's got legs. May's well learn from the start which way they'll be leading him." So the boy was half-led, half-dragged with his arm held vertical by the man's fist, towards the new workplaces that even on Sundays were filled with the subdued beating of engines. Out here his father cursed freely, inviting the boy into a man's fellowship of work and sweat. "Tired, kid? I bloody bet y'are. T's how it is. T's how it's always been for them like us." He turned the boy's face towards each factory in turn. "But we're winnin, kid. We made our claim, an look!"

After the singing, long silence and the dark. Her body trembling, sudden outbursts of her breath. She clenched him tight, tighter, till he slithered from her grip with,

"Mam! I cannot breathe."

"Where's that man? she whispered. "Stephen, go and look."

At the door he followed with his eyes the curve of streetlights, shadowed gardens, curtained panes.

She shouted at him, "Well? Well?" She came up beside him, shoved his arms into a coat.

"Thinks we're nothin. Thinks he can do it, like he said he would. Can't, can he? Can't get away with it. We'll find the bugger, Stephen, bloody right we will. Out you go. Come on, bloody out!"

Out through an alleyway onto the dead straight road leading to the crest, cutting across a waste of weedy underfill toward the darkened factories. Nothing but a thin whining from them now, padlocked gates, massive loading doors sealed shut. At his place, beneath its shattered neon name, the one light came from a shed at arm's length inside the fence. She shoved her arm through, hammered at it. From inside a man's voice yelled at her to clear off home. She went on hammering, until its tiny window was opened and he yelled,

"Is that still you sodding kids?"

"It's me," she told him. "Me. Look. Just me, an the lad here."

He angled his head through the open frame.

"What's wrong, woman? What you after?"

"Me man," she said. "I'm lookin for me man."

"Oh, aye?"

"I want to know who's workin," she said. "If he's workin."

"Workin? No bugger, only me. They finished ages past."

"But if there's another shift... If they needed one to get it done... "

"Look around, woman. Listen."

She pressed her face hard against the fence.

"Then where is he? Where's my man?"

The watchman stared at her. He sighed and spat.

"Go home, woman. There's more to worry him than bloody silly women an their kids."

The window slammed. They headed back to the estate. On the wasteland in between she picked up half-bricks, stones, and flung them out into the dark. Afterwards, they searched the pubs, didn't find him there.

Feathers and cotton clung to his skin. He drew his knees to his chest, squirmed into the rags. He was so cold. He would have to move.

He'd dreamed of going home one night to find her dying, the house ransacked, the bloodied snooker cue beside her head. But tonight was like most nights: opening the door to a room filled with the fierce heat of a gas fire, to her drunken sleep; leaving her there, going to stare from his window at the ring of lights surrounded by the dark; slipping towards unconsciousness again, towards the memory of his father, the last night he'd come in...

"Stevie! Stevie!" An urgent whisper, the man leaning over him, the door open to the landing's glare.

"Stevie! What's the matter wi'ye?"

Blinking, heart thundering, gasping for air.

"Stevie! It's me, lad. What's up wi'ye?"

"Nothin." A garbled cry.

"So what ye laughin for?"

"Laughin? Dream, dad…Must've been a dream."

"Bugger dreams, lad. Sleep, lad. Eh?"

"Yes, dad."

"No dreams now, eh?"

"No, Dad…"

The man turning to leave, but hesitating, pushing the door to, returning through the darkness to the bed. Crouching low, his lips hard by the boy's ear, his whisper cracking with it's angry edge,

"This is how they get you, this is how they lie to you. Look at this, they tell you. Isn't it grand, isn't it what you've always wanted? Get you when you're daft, half-asleep, when they tell you, Good lad, always knew you were a good'n. Gan on, they say, Smile. Look what we've got you. Gan on, lad, take it…Bastards! Get you when you're dreaming, son, get you when you're soft. And not long till they've got what they wanted and they're telling you, No! Leave off! Get back to where you were! Back in your box, bird brain. Yours? Wors. Wors all the time. Not for the like o'you. Piss off back to sleep. Leave it!…You know what I'm saying son?"

Stephen lay as if he couldn't move, breathing low, his heart racing.

"Get out, Stevie. That's me meanin. That's the thing to do. Get out quick's you can. Soon as there's a space, start runnin. They'll try to stop you. Nice lad, they'll say. Always been a good'n. Come here, look at this, they'll say. Don't believe them, Stevie. Tell them, Stevie: Piss off wi'your lies! Aye? Stevie!"

Huge hands gripped Stephen's head, twisted it round towards the dark face.

"Stevie! Tell me aye. Bloody aye!"

"Yes…yes…aye…," the words coming suddenly on each panted breath.

"Good lad, Stevie. That's the way. When they come to you, just tell them no."

The hands relaxed. The face dipped towards him, kissed him.

"Good lad. You'll be all right. Just gan to sleep. That's right, son. That's right…love."

Nothing more, except, as the man moved towards the door, the final words, "An don't marry. Don't fall for that lot, either;" and later, the ferocious voices of both of them, man and woman, stretching deep into the night.

"...an he'd lean over, from where you're sittin now, an he'd lay his whole hand across me belly – like this, look. Just to feel you. Just to feel the kickin of you. An he'd swear – you know, the way he did. Bugger, he'd say. Feel it growin, gettin strong. He'd keep on askin, How big's it, how big's it now? An when he'd had a drink he'd come an lay his head on me and he'd whisper at you and whistle for you. He'd be that daft – like a kid that cannot wait. Howay, little'n, he'd say. Howay out an play wi'us. You never knew him, Stephen – not when he was young and full of everythin. I've got it all, he used to say, an, Me an you, love, we've got it all..."

Mornings were calm, comparatively lucid. When the sun shone and the blackbirds sang, she'd lift a table into the small back garden and they'd breakfast there, facing each other, their knees almost touching. Her words each time searched the same themes: the past, his father, the building of the estate and the factories. But her stories had never become tedious to him. Though he never met her eyes, and hardly spoke except to mutter yes or no when asked if he, too, remembered, he was alert to every word, bringing as it did some answer to his prompting of years ago: Tell me what it was like...

"...it was spring when you were growin fastest. Felt some days like you were takin all the strength from me, an all I could do was lie and let him fuss round me. Days when I was stronger he'd take me out onto the waggonways an we'd walk an walk, right down past the tips an dumps. What a change there'd be down there, where you could lose yourself in the lanes an hedges. It was the silence of it all, when up here there was all day long the trucks an drills an engines. An wi'th plans they had, seemed like it would go on always, like there'd be no stop to it, like the estates would just keep spreadin an spreadin...But it were'nt to be...Comin back, I'd have to hold him tight, let him take me weight. Take it easy, love, he'd say. An he'd let me stop an get me breath while he climbed right into the hedges lookin for nests an shouting back about the eggs an little'ns he'd found. An many's the time I came back here wi'a warm hedge-sparrow's egg in me hand or a chaffinch's in me pocket..."

Her voice faded. Soon, he knew, it would deepen, she'd begin to search her other theme, of how it all went wrong. She held him as he tried to move away.

"We watched you growin straight an strong and he'd laugh an say, The jammy sod – born now, best of all times to be born..."

From inside, through the kitchen window, he watched her head fall forward. He shivered. She'd start on the bad times, the changes. "It broke his heart, Stevie. It changed him. It started him sayin we shouldn't've started any of it, we shouldn't've met, we shouldn't've come here. He started watchin you an sayin we shouldn't've had you, it might all have been easier if we hadn't've had you..."

"Stevie!" She had turned to him, and he saw that the morning's light hadn't entirely drained from her eyes. "An your eggs! You remember them? Boxes an boxes o'them underneath your bed. All that bright blue an the white an the dark patches. An how he loved you even then? How he'd sit wi'you an hold them wi'you and keep tellin you what this one was an this one was..."

"Aye," said Stephen, moving from the window, heading out. He did remember – the man's gentle touch as he fingered the hollow shells and the pinholes; how he turned his face from the boy as he muttered that this was maybe the best way,

"Spat out like so much snot – never to be born at all."

Some days he still went out like this, as if he were still dragged by his father's fist. He ascended the hill, passed the silent factories, squatted among the heather and rocks at the crest. He kept jamming a tin of lighter fluid to his nostril, squeezing. Icy-cold, breath-stopping, but with an almost immediate thrill that sent his mind reeling. The estate hunched in on itself behind back gardens and fences. The broken ground at its fringes contained trenches and heaps of under-fill, remnants of long-abandoned building projects, weeds that each spring were higher and more dense. He saw his father's arms widening as he described what was to come, filling the space with houses and workplaces going on for ever. He saw his father in a rage, coming out from the factories, running to the crest, setting off on the miles-long ribbon of road towards the city, yelling, "No. Bloody no!" One day he'd follow him...Thin mucous was draining from him. He sniffed, spat. He'd said no, months ago. They'd come to him, wanting him for their schemes and projects, with, "He's a good lad, is Stephen. We'll train him. We'll give him what he needs." He watched them, silent. Lies, he thought. They were tender, telling him he'd change things for his mother and himself. She'd been with him, had turned to him, her eyes widening with anticipation. "No!" he'd yelled at her. "Bloody no!"...He spat again. He stood up, began his descent. All across the hillside the work of those who'd said yes was starting: neat signposts at the junction of the waggonways, trimmed and newly-laid hedges, turfed spoil heaps. They'd get to his cottage, raze it. They'd clear the estate's fringes. There'd be playgrounds and pic-nic spots. On the crest there'd be parking places and benches. Chil-dren on tiptoe would peer through telescopes as far as the sea. You could be part of all this, they'd told him. You'll help the whole place to be reborn. People will want this place, will want you to come. "Stephen," she'd whispered – her whining voice. "No!" he'd yelled. "Bloody no!"...He veered past the estate onto his familiar cindered track. He started when the hedge started. He ducked into the dark, climbed, balanced in the forks of the boughs, peered towards the tips, heard all around him the mothers, filled with fright, clattering towards the sky. Nests; so many of them, deep inside the foliage, held and protected by spreading twigs and branches. He stretched, reached up, dipped his fingers into the first: a blackbird's with its smooth and cupped inside. Three eggs. He lifted them one by one, placed them gently into his free hand's open palm. For a moment he regarded them, their blueness, their dark speckles. For a moment he heard the familiar voice from below: *In your mouth, lad. Rest it on your tongue where it's warm and safe.* He closed his fist tight. He sniffed, wiped his hand on his clothes, began again. The nests he couldn't reach he brought down, kicking and wrenching the branches that supported them until they splintered and snapped. He moved slowly stepping from tree to tree, balancing, staring, reaching. All afternoon he worked. Occasionally he rested, squatting in a wide fork and holding the lighter fluid to his nose. Once, in a strong tree, he climbed so high that his head emerged from the foliage and he stared back, saw how short a space, compared with the miles of hedgerow that crossed the slope, he'd dealt with. But he didn't relent, went back into the dark, went back to leaving the ground and the branches scattered with smashed eggs, with young birds cheeping uselessly for their parents, went back to telling himself, "Better like this. Aye, better like this..."

At dusk, he dropped to the track. He marked the place with a pile of stones. He shuffled through to his cottage, curled up in there. His clothes were ripped, his skin torn. Tiny fragments of shell had attached themselves to every part of him. He took out the lighter fluid once more. Nothing left except a vapour. It brought no thrill.

He didn't reel. But he slept, and entered a darkness deeper than any there'd ever been out here in the waste; darkness with the thudding of blood in it and with a voice from outside coming closer, asking, "How big's it? How big's it now?" and going on to call him, "Little'n! Little'n! Howay out an play wi'us…"

They hadn't come. There was no bloodied snooker cue. She was sleeping on the sofa, facing the gas fire. He stood staring, this boy coated with shell and feathers and with hollow eyes. He didn't want to leave, didn't want the whisper or the landing's glare. She didn't move. He turned off the light, turned off the fire, lay down with her. Without waking, she moved to accommodate him, allowed him to curl up close against her belly. They stayed all night. He kept waking. He kept promising her,

"I'll protect you, Mam. I'll stay inside…"

Observations From The Outside Toilet

When a child discovers an important secret about an adult, the revelation is both exciting and awesome. It represents power but also responsibility, for with the desire to boast of one's knowledge comes the realization that one risks the whirlwind of reprisal when the taboos of age and hypocrisy are exposed. I had discovered such a secret and the implications were so enormous that I locked myself in the outside toilet. I had meant to sit there for a few minutes to review the possibilities, but the wind moved the wooden catch on the door and I was trapped for two hours.

"What do you use this dirty place for?" my Grandma demanded when she released me. Her eyes checked the whitewashed walls to make sure I had not been writing rude words. "We don't use this one any more. You use the inside one see."

I looked at her carefully. Should I tell her my secret, or just ask a few innocent questions?

"Now you get off to your Uncle Vernon's, he needs some help with the apple picking; and stop hiding in the toilet, only mouchins do that."

The moment had passed and I kept silent.

My Grandma was a strong woman; short, stocky and with grey, thoughtful eyes. I often felt that she knew more about me than I considered proper. Whenever I had the chance of visiting a travelling funfair or racing snails with my cousin Roy, she would always have a letter for me to write or a list of spellings to learn. When I wished to play checquers with Grandpa, she would suggest Lexicon. She seemed to know when I wanted to 'waste time', as she put it, and there was always a job to do or an errand to run that would occupy most of the morning.

"The devil finds work for idle hands," she would say. I would mutter that I never had the chance to meet him.

She believed in regular baths, hair washing in the kitchen sink, never locking doors and church on Sunday. On the last point she made a concession that I could go with Grandpa to the Hope Chapel instead of church, but only providing I brushed my hair and made my Grandpa proud of me. Anything was better than the moral interrogation of Grandpa's female cabal.

My grandparents were kind but strict. There was order, tradition and uneventful habit. It was possible to predict almost to the minute the movements of each day. They were both strict tee-totallers, and

Grandma would often point out the picture of an old man in tattered clothes raising a bottle to his lips, with the fainter outline of a young handsome and well-dressed youth in the background.

"See what happens when you drink," she would say pointing forcibly at the old man. "Never touch strong drink boy, and never go near a public house now."

One time I had been foolish enough to ask why and had been treated to a seemingly unending list of close relatives who had been destroyed or ruined by the demon drink. "Never let me hear of you drinking or you will end up a dirty old man like your Uncle Harold." I was impressed.

Sunday was the day of sublime predictability. The call at eight... into my best suit...a walk with Grandpa to collect the Sunday Express, then back for a cooked breakfast. At the end of the meal Grandpa would announce to his empty teacup: "I must count the money in the shop. I don't want to be disturbed." Then, after consulting his pocket watch in a distsracted way, he would disappear downstairs to his large drapers shop and lock the door.

The house was enormous, and I would position myself in one of the bay windows and watch the stirrings in the street below. I always hoped that a beautiful girl would glide along and wave to me, but the most excitement I observed was the Jones' dog peeing on Mr Bevan's milk bottles. After an hour Grandma would appear. "Tell your Grandpa it's time for chapel, and make sure you have something for collection." I was supposed to give some of my pocket money, but I usually managed to forget and Grandpa would contribute for me.

I made my way down the wide staircase to the dark corridor which connected the shop to the front and back entrances and hammered loudly on the old oak door. The stuffed heads of a stag and a Cape Buffalo frowned down and I always expected some hideous creature to burst out from the cellars behind me. Grandpa would emerge with much rattling of keys and would hand me a bag of sweets. "Have a peppermint...make you grow big and strong." He was always very cheerful when he had counted his money. We then walked up the main street to the Hope Chapel where Grandpa checked in the motley congregation of fifteen; roared out the hymns – more ancient than modern, and snored in a defiant manner throughout the sermon. On the way back we chewed more peppermints.

On Sunday evening he produced his stamp album, full of first sets from countries that no longer existed: Fiume, Latvia and Abyssinia. The names seemed mysterious and conjured up visions of wild men and lost civilisations. Grandpa had hundreds of Victorian stamps, and I turned the pages with fascinated reverence as Penny Blacks and Reds were spread out before me. Grandma broke the spell: "Time for bed now boy. Say goodnight to your Grandpa." Unwillingly I moved from the table.

"We'll look at the stamps again tomorrow." Grandpa murmured and closed the album. I climbed the long staircase up to the lino-covered landing. My room had two pictures: one of a woman in flowing robes embracing a large rock surrounded by a raging sea. The caption read: "Only to thy rock I cling". The other was of a single rose with the message: "God hates the drunkard". I lay in bed searching the pictures for any new feature; there was none. I counted the squares on the lino and as I drifted into sleep, I vowed that I would spend the whole of the next day examining the stamp album.

At first light I crept down to the breakfast room. It was cold and shadowy and there was no sign of the album. In the kitchen I could hear my Grandma washing her hair in the sink next to the pantry. She would use only rain water, which she collected in a butt in the garden. She had done this ever since childhood, and it was similar to the way she scrubbed herself with seaweed when we went to the beach, always oblivious to the stares of the summer visitors. Grandma did not change with fashion; she still wore the revealing woollen bathing costume of thirty years before, and kept milk in jugs in the pantry even though my uncle had bought her a fridge.

"Have you seen Grandpa's stamp album?" I asked her.

"He locks it away; it's valuable see," she said as she manouvered me towards the sink. "I'll wash your hair now before breakfast." My protests were loud but in vain.

Later when Grandpa appeared for breakfast, I resembled the colour of a clean pink lobster, my skin raw with rubbing. He seemed preoccupied and a dew drop formed at the end of his nose. I rested my chin on my hands and watched to see if it would fall in his tea.

"Percy! Wipe your nose, man, for shame," Grandma said. I felt cheated as his handkerchief removed the first pendulous drip.

"Grandpa, can I look at your album?"

"Tonight boy, you can see it tonight." Without a glance in my direction he left the room.

Later that morning I returned from an errand to see Grandpa standing at the open door chatting to an old man with huge ears and a walking stick. I slipped past them into the empty shop. Long polished counters and high stools marked the perimeters of the customers' area, behind these were glass-fronted drawers, rolls of materials and racks of clothes. My Uncle was contemplating a crossword, my Aunt was rearranging one of the window displays and Gwyneth, the trainee salesgirl, was biting her nails in a dreamy, love-sick way. Nobody noticed me.

I sauntered round the corner to Grandpa's inner sanctum: a small office that said "Private" on the door. Nobody was allowed in this small square room, not even Grandma ventured in, and the door was kept locked. "Because the safe is in there see," Grandpa had explained.

As no one could see me, I turned the handle and the door opened. My heart was thudding and my mouth had gone suddenly dry, but I was determined to find the album and I darted quickly inside, closing the door softly behind me. On the leather-topped desk was a pile of books and papers. I searched the cluttered shelves, noticing the old photographs on the wall and the faded certificates for life-saving and dog-shows. There was no sign of the album.

I sat down cautiously on the padded revolving chair and prayed that the stamps were not locked in the safe. I pushed back my hair; there was sweat on my brow. I stared at the two rows of drawers; they were closed except for a large one on the right hand side which was slightly askew. To explore a closed drawer seemed a terrible crime, but to delve into one that was already open was permissible. Quickly I pulled the drawer out, but there was no album. I was so disappointed that I almost failed to see what was there.

My Grandma's words beat in my brain like a loud drum. I stared in disbelief. It was like looking at a bomb or finding a cow pat on the breakfast table, I did not know what to do about it. I was looking at a half-empty bottle of Scotch Whisky. Replacing the drawer, I fled to the outside toilet.

Dorothy Nimmo

Landscape With Nude Figures

I am bent double creeping out of the van. The children are still asleep, James is still asleep. I am wearing flowered pyjamas. It gets cold at night, you can tell by the heavy dew weighing down the long grasses beside the dirt path to the latrine block. I didn't know if it was all right to wear pyjamas. They were quite stern about alcohol and meat and cigarettes and if you wore your tracksuit, even if it was chilly, there would always be someone to make encouraging gestures urging you to strip off. They would wave, heave their muscular bronzed shoulders, shout in German or French or English, "Feel the air on your body! Feel the good sun!"

But I thought, well no-one can see what I wear at night, I don't like sleeping naked. James, I think would like me to sleep naked but I don't like it. He is just so hot. I don't know if all men are hot, I have never slept with any other man. I had never seen any other man naked before we came to the camp. No-one had ever seen me naked either, except for that time with Estelle, at the Turkish Bath.

But at school, you will say, surely at school? All those girls? But no, we always tried not to be completely naked. We would undress under our tunics, wriggling out of our knickers with our top halves still covered, bundling our pyjama bottoms up under our skirts. Then we would sling our dressing-gowns over our shoulders while we stripped out of our blouses, vests and bras, faces to the wall, backs to the dormitory. We kept our bodies neatly under our uniforms and our selves inside our bodies all through those years.

There had been procedures to be gone through before they would let us in to the camp. We had to apply for membership, fill in a form stating age, sex, marital status, reason for applying and how had we first become interested in Naturism? Age: mid-twenties. Sex: male and female. Occupation: him, International Marketing Specialist. Her: none. SANS PROFESSION was what they wrote down. We are married, we have two children. And why, they asked, did we want to join the Sun Club? In the upstairs room of a restaurant, confronting several tightly buttoned Swiss James answered. His French is fluent. Something to do with wanting the children to grow up free of foolish damaging inhibitions, something about harmony with nature. Yes, we were vegetarians, he told them, we did not drink or smoke, we believed in alternative medicine and positive health. Something like that. It wasn't all true but James was an advertising man.

Out of the van I search around with my bare cold foot and find my plastic sandal. I push my toes between the thongs; my big toe joint is slightly deformed from wearing pointed shoes when they were fashionable. I draw my pyjama top up over my head and push it inside the van behind the seat cushions. Polly and Jane are beginning to stir and snort. I pull my pyjama bottoms down my thighs, get my feet entangled in the elastic, steady myself and step out of them. James does not move, he is all snarled up in the sleeping bag. I stand upright. My waist is marked with the elastic of my pyjama bottoms and a button has imprinted itself on my left breast. I hope no-one is up so early, to notice that I have been sleeping in pyjamas. All the other tents are zipped close but over there, across the grass, there is an enclosure behind a little picket fence, a vegetable plot and there is an old man bending over cabbage plants. He straightens himself and looks in my direction. I duck my head and fold myself up to pick up something imaginary from under my sandal strap. When I unfold he waves at me. I pretend not to see him but I do see him, stretching his arms towards the pale sky, smiling between his raised arms, nodding. He is telling me it will be a fine day when the mist clears and the dew dries up. It will be hot. He is swinging his arms vigorously now, and bending to touch his toes. Now he picks up a red plastic watering can and moves off towards the tap. His shins are knotted and hairy above his heavy boots. He stops suddenly, sets the can down and stoops to pick something from a cabbage leaf. As he crouches his back towards me, I see his buttocks are triangular, boney, and between his thighs the soft fall of his wrinkley old scrotum. He drops whatever it is into his palm, I see his fingers curl over it as he moves over to the boundary hedge. He crouches, flattening his palm for it to crawl away.

I wipe the dew from the camping table. A woman comes to the door of the wooden hut opposite our van, submerged in a pile of bedding. She arranges it on the railing of the little terrace. Her thin body on its little thin legs is deep brown all over. She picks up a water container and starts down the path towards the tap, pausing as she passes me, smiling.

"Charlotte," she says, introducing herself, "a beautiful day!" She offers a hand.

"Anna," I say, laying down cornflakes and yoghurt to take it. We smile. We do not exchange our full names; one does not.

"Beautiful children!" says Charlotte.

Polly and Jane have clambered out of the van, their nightdresses rucked up under their armpits.

"Take your nighties off, girls!"

But they sit on the van step pulling their nighties down over their knees.

"It's cold!" says Polly.

I look apologetically at Charlotte.

"They will become accustomed," she says, "it is the first time?"

"Yes," I say. But she could tell easily by my stark white breasts and buttocks.

"You must take care, the first time," she says, "Go by little and little, it is easy to get burned."

Her belly has folded down over her pubis; she is so thin you can see the socket of her hip. When my Aunt Lily was dying she sat in her chair like a very small tortoise, her neck withering into her cardy, her hands like claws under the thick hand-knit cuffs, her tiny ankles wreathed in loops of stocking. She used to get very fierce because of the pain. Charlotte is stark naked, she is very mild and pleasant but I cannot avoid recognising the pain.

Outside the latrine block a group are assembled for their morning gymnastics. A young woman directs them with sharp insistent cries. Twenty people bend and stretch, bend and stretch, jump up and down, their breasts and penises flapping. There is a serious incongruity between their nakedness and those deliberate artificial movements. I don't like to look at them. Now they all lie on the hard dew-wet grass lifting their legs in the air, once, twice, three times. The wirey grass prints their thighs.

As the morning wears on and the sun strengthens a procession of people thread their way along a mud path between reed beds to the lake. At the water's edge they wade through the reeds, their feet sinking in mud. Polly and Jane baulk at what may be lurking in the mud but I urge them on. They stand in the water, dark verticals, their shins rippling the water into bright flecks. All round, in the shallows, mothers are splashing their children's shoulders and bellies, dashing handfuls of water over the brown skin. And fathers, having laved their hairy armpits and chests, lower themselves and swim, keeping their heads high.

"It's lovely," I say, with that determined confidence with which I approach things I am afraid the children may not enjoy. Polly and Jane wade in deeper, gain courage, paddle their hands, submerge themselves and swim.

Lying flat, floating in the water I see ripples, I see reedbeds against the sky, I see the further shore of the lake. The water is warm and shallow, the reeds stroke my flesh. I tell myself as I tell the children that the water is lovely but I am taking care to keep my mouth closed.

At mid-day someone comes out of the centre block and beats with a spoon on a saucepan. "MIT-TAG-ESS-EN!" she shouts, her voice ringing out over the lake. From the tents, the caravans, the chalets, people emerge, uncurling, stretching. They rouse themselves from where they have been spread out in the sun, return along the path from the lake, from under the showers, towelling themselves vigorously. All morning there have been women at the table outside the camp office grating carrots, cutting up tomatoes. Now they stand behind the table and ladle out salads. I see Charlotte holding out her plate, accepting a spoonful of this, a spoonful of that. She covers her plate with a cloth and balances it carefully, stepping gingerly because the path through the long grass under the trees is still damp. She sits on her terrace to eat but she eats little.

"Good pure food!" she tells us, nodding, gesticulating over the grass, "Is good! Is Nature's food!"

Polly and Jane, hungry after their swim, have found crisps, peanuts, a bottle of Coke. Charlotte lifts her face to the sun, the good sun to which she has exposed herself every summer. She and her husband and the children used to come every summer, she tells us, but they are grown up now and her husband no longer with them it is two years now. But they came every summer and grew up strong and free in the good sunshine. Outside her little wooden chalet Charlotte is nursing her body towards its end. And I can see her. So I shut my eyes, feeling the sun on my eyelids, on my body, comforting and treacherous. The cells of my skin thicken, colour, mutate.

"Could you throw me a t-shirt, James," I say, "I think I've had enough sun for today."

Under the trees a great wheel lies on its side. Two men lift it with shouts, "Ah!" they cry with the effort, and "Hup!" It is like the open-work iron wheels they fit to tractors so they can work the wet ground without compacting the soil. Six feet high, a double wheel, the sort they provide for small animals confined in cages so they can run and run, hoping to escape, but the wheel turns round and they stay where they are. This wheel is as tall as a man; now a tall man stands, feet straddling three rungs, arms spread, hands clutching the rungs above his head. It is James, tempting fate. I watch him, I am concerned that he may not be able to move the wheel. There were a couple of small boys playing on it earlier who couldn't shift it and later an old man wearing only socks and gym-shoes had spread himself out, strained this way and that so that the wheel swung but didn't swing right round so the youths on the volley-ball court jeered at him. James wouldn't like it if they jeered. There he is, spreadeagled, Polly and Jane staring up at him. He bends his knees, he pulls the rungs above his head, right arm, left arm, this way, that way and the wheel shifts. His weight shifts the wheel swinging it further over with each pressure of the thigh, each downward pull of a shoulder until now finally it unbalances, turns right round, rolls over and over across the grass with James now upright, now hanging upside down, his hair hanging like a fright wig. He is Saint Sebastian and if I were to take up an arrow, aim and throw I could pierce him right in the centre. There.

I wouldn't do it. James is so pleased with himself that he has succeeded in swinging the wheel that he takes Polly and Jane for an icecream.

There used to be a Turkish Bath in Jermyn Street. Estelle said, "Let's go. I've never been to a Turkish Bath."

I said, "Oh well. I don't know." But I went with her. She had long red hair, we shared a flat. She was like a lion. Her face was not beautiful but it was proud because she had this long red curly hair. We went to the Mens Entrance first and they laughed at us but Estelle didn't care. She was a Socialist, she cared for nothing, she said, but justice. At election time she would go round knocking on people's doors, asking them to vote Labour and if they banged the door in her face she didn't care. She would laugh and swing her long red hair about. Estelle would have been ashamed to be afraid of anything.

When we found the right door we went in and they gave us very small towels to wrap round ourselves. We left our clothes in the cubicles and went and sat on these slatted boards in a haze of disinfectant steam. You couldn't see anything clearly. The walls were green tiles, running with water. I held the little towel close round me though it hardly covered me. There were women lying on the benches, their breasts and buttocks spilling all over the place. One of them said, "Take your towel off, you must not be ashamed of your body!"

"I'm not," I said.

"Why are you holding your towel like that?" she said, "There is nothing to be afraid of. Let it go! Feel free!"

As I let the towel go she looked at me.

When we had been in the hot room and the cold room and the steam room we went to the massage room and a woman massaged us. She had big strong hands. Then she took me to another room where she aimed jets of water at me, and then there was a deep pool of warm water and she said, "Now you can have a swim." Estelle jumped straight into the water. She was naked in the water with that white skin and her hair floating all gold in the water until it got wet and dark, slicked down her back.

"Oh," said Estelle, "It's so warm! Come on, what are you waiting for? Jump!"

I curled my toes round the rubber rim of the pool and clutched my towel.

It's quite awkward to be mother naked all day long. Just imagine, in the camp shop, how large and intrusive are the buttocks of the lady who bends over a box of tomatoes to pick out the firm ones. Imagine the arm-pit of the man stretching up for a tin of olives, how the rusty-coloured crinkley hair springs from the hollow between the tendons. Imagine the bellies you have to push past on your way to the cash desk. Excuse me, you say, if you happen to touch but it seems inadequate. How absurd we are queuing up with our wire baskets resting against our bare thighs. How foolish our handbags seem, slung across our nakedness. We ignore the absurdity and hardly notice the effort it takes to ignore it.

Down by the water's edge, on a small strip of shingle, we lie on our mats and watch him stroll by. His red neck and weathered forearms contrast with his white body so that you know at once that he has not exposed himself before. He spreads a towel and sits, rubbing oil into his shoulders and chest.

"English?" he says, hopefully, overhearing Polly and Jane fighting over their rubber ring. We agree we are English. "My first time here," he says.

"Ah," we say.

"Not bad," he says, rubbing oil into his belly. He says, "What I want to know is, what I wondered was. Well," he says, not looking at us. He seriously wants to know, his words come out jerky, urgent. "What do you do when? What do I do, well, what happens when a man, well, when he gets his nature up?" He rolls over on his stomach, just in case.

"It doesn't happen," says James.

"Not?" he says, doubtfully.

"No," says James decisively.

We are a little uncomfortable now we are back in our clothes. We have got a bit burnt in the places we are not accustomed to expose, the slope of the buttocks, the top of the breasts. Though we have been careful. It is nice to be dressed again. It is really nice to be hidden safely away under our clothes. All our household gear is stowed away in the van, we have put away the vegetable rack, the watercan, the buckets and balls and books, the rubber ring, the table, the chairs, the pink plastic potty. We have hardly noticed, though we feel it now it is over, the effort it has been to live so exposed. Polly's nightmares have woken old Charlotte early in the morning, Jane's undisciplined screams under the shower have echoed across the camp; the Germans have disapproved. We have stood in the queue for the lavatory in the morning. We have noticed, as people passed and repassed our van, how they registered the disorder, the lack of discipline. I have felt their eyes rest on my slack belly and have held myself in as they went by.

Now my stomach is held in safely under my jeans, my breasts are comfortingly supported by my bra and James steers the van out through the gates of the camp, up the rough track along the river. All along the banks we see family parties, men standing by the river casting fishing lines, children playing. Now we see a woman standing knee deep in the reeds; her hands are clamped over her ears. She is screaming. We can't hear her scream because we are in the van, the engine is running and the windows are shut but we can see her mouth is open. Her hands move from her ears to her mouth, then they are above her head waving. We have already driven past but the picture remains very clear and bright. There was activity somewhere on the periphery of the scene which we couldn't make sense of at the time. Did we see children sitting by a picnic basket laid on the grass? Were they screaming too? Was there an empty boat in the middle of the river? Someone may have been swimming, perhaps towards the boat?

We saw the paragraph in the local paper later. How a man had been fishing, his wife and children picnicking nearby. A respected man, from Neuchatel just up the road. He ran a garage and was prominent in local affairs, a socialist, much involved in charitable works, middle-aged, his wife a local girl, his children still young. He would be much missed. His line, they surmised had got caught up in the reeds, he had been to pull, trying to get it free and then to jerk and overbalance into the water. His wife waited for him to surface. He was a good swimmer. It was some few minutes before she became alarmed. She waded out as far as she could but saw no trace of him. That was when she had screamed. Someone called the pompiers who dragged the river. He was discovered some yards downstream caught up in the reeds. Sympathy would go out to the bereaved family.

It was as if we hadn't been able to bear to look any more. I had had to make such an effort not to be sensitive, not to respond, not to react that I couldn't make it any more. I had had simply to stop looking. I had put my clothes back on, covered myself up and shut my eyes.

And that man really drowned as we drove past.

DAVID ALMOND was born in Felling-on-Tyne in 1951. He was educated on Tyneside and at the University of East Anglia. He began writing in his late twenties, and his fiction has appeared in many magazines and anthologies, including *Bananas, Iron, Argo* and *Prospice*. His first collection of short stories, *'Sleepless Nights'* was published in 1985 by *Iron Press*. He has worked in adult literacy, special education, and as a tutor for the Arvon Foundation. He lives in Newcastle-upon-Tyne, and is Editor of the twice-yearly fiction magazine *'Panurge'*.

ARTHUR APPLETON writes as follows: Left school in Sunderland in 1928 when 14. Later stockbrokers' clerk, Youth Hostel Warden, engineering shop worker, sergeant in the Royal Engineers and Forces Broadcasting Service, Middle East, and 27 years with the BBC as reporter, sub editor and producer. Author of six non-fiction books – one, *Mary Ann Cotton*, a crime biography; a score of radio features and three television features. Also 22 short stories broadcast nationally or published. A collection of them, *The Ice-cold Revenge of John Dolan (Iron Press)*, came out last year. Reports on soccer for the Sunday Times.

M. ASLETT lives in Whitburn, near Sunderland, Tyne and Wear.

CAROL BARKER was born in Amersham in 1960 and later moved north to Leeds, where she took a degree in English Literature at the University. She now lives in Otley in Wharfedale. She has been writing for several years and her short stories have been published in *P.E.N. New Fiction II (Quartet Books)* and broadcast on *Morning Story* on BBC Radio Four.

PAT BINCE writes: I am 58 years old and have carried the writing itch since I was about 10. I have had some stories and poetry published in small magazines and one story was read in the BBC's 'Morning Story' slot. Having recently stopped working, I am trying to write a novel. Apart from that, I am short, reasonably cheerful, house trained and moderately well behaved.

DAVID CRAIG writes: Born Aberdeen 1932. 1 daughter and 3 sons. Lives with Anne Spillard in Cumbria. Taught in NE of Scotland schools, University of Ceylon, North Yorkshire WEA, and now teaches Creative Writing (under and post-graduate) in the University of Lancaster. Books include (poems) *Latest News* (with Ken Sprague: Journeyman) and *Against Looting* (Giant Steps); (novel) *The Rebels And The Hostage* (with Nigel Gray: Journeyman) and *King Cameron* (forthcoming: Carcanet); *Native Stones* (Secker); several books of criticism; and 3 literary texts edited for Penguin. Now working on a 'historical travel book' about the Highland Clearances for Secker.

CHRIS FIRTH writes: Male. Hopelessly addicted to writing from the age of 12. Bradford-born. Aged 25. Attended Sheffield Poly as they had 'creative writing' combined with English Degree – tutor, Barry Hines encouraged me to stick to writing. Recently qualified as teacher, but am going on Enterprise Allowance as 'Script-Writer' to enable full-time writing. 1985 – Yorkshire Arts Bursary. first novel *'Lilacs'* second in Constable Trophy Competition. Presently writing second novel *'Yahoo'*, and polishing short story collection for London agent.

ROBERT FORSTER (41) was born into rural Northumberland. One of his early memories was being forbidden access to a Shorthorn bull penned in secure isolation on his God Parent's farm. And as a schoolboy he became familiar with a huge, black, bull that was well respected locally for its size and its temper. Later as a civilian administrator in remote Papua New Guinea he came across a group of Goilala tribesmen who had failed to kill a bull despite being in possession of an overworked .22 rifle. He has since returned to the Hexham area of Northumberland and now works as livestock correspondent for the nationally distributed weekly, 'Farmers Guardian'.

ALISON GUINANE writes: I was born in 1948, in Manchester, where my parents lived and worked all their lives. Their stories, their language, and their grasp of reality have influenced me a great deal. I went to University in York, my first child was born in Derbyshire, and then I lived in London for a while, but I returned to Manchester when my marriage ended. I was married for five years and had three babies, two of which were born dead – an experience which has often inspired my writing. I now live with my eighteen-year-old daughter, and teach English at a Sixth Form College.

PAULINE KEITH grew up in Bolton and graduated from Leicester before leaving for jobs in the Middle and Far East, West Africa, Holland and Canada. Since returning to the north-west with her son and daughter, she has lived in Lancaster. She helped to establish the Lancaster Literature Festival and has recently completed David Craig's M.A. in Creative Writing at Lancaster University. She works as a lecturer at W.R. Turson College, Preston. Individual poems have appeared in various magazines and small groups in 'Giant Steps No 8' and the 'Rivelin Grapheme' anthology 'Purple and Green'.

JOHN LATHAM writes: Middle-aged physicist. Tutor to Arvon Foundation at Lumb Bank and Totleigh Barton. Two collections of poetry published by Harry Chambers' Peterloo Poets: 'Unpacking Mr Jones' (1982) and 'From the Other Side of the Street' (1985). Third collection: 'All Clear' due out in 1989. Won several poetry competitions. Various poems anthologised or broadcast. One radio play broadcast on 'Afternoon Theatre' (BBC Radio 4, 1988), and short stage-play produced at Royal Exchange Theatre, 1987. A few short stories published, most recently in Prospice and Critical Quarterly. A novel is bouncing inexhaustibly around publishers and agencies. No operas.

ALISON MACLEOD was born in Montreal in 1964 and grew up in Halifax on Canada's eastern coast. She obtained her first degree, in English, in 1985. In 1987 she moved to England on acceptance to the University of Lancaster's M.A. programme in creative writing. To date she has written several short stories, a television script, and is currently completing her first novel.

BARRY MATHIAS is aged 46, married with two daughters and living in a small village north of York. He is of Anglo-Welsh extraction and much influenced by his Celtic roots. He is Head of English at a Comprehensive School. He has lived in the area for fifteen years and is a regular visitor to Arvon. He writes short stories, often autobiographical and set in Wales, some of which have been read on local radio. He has also written drama sketches, reviews and two plays which have been performed at school and at local venues. He is writing a novel for teenagers and plays for radio.

GRAHAM MORT was born in Middleton, Lancashire in 1955. He has written four books of poetry: 'A Country on Fire' (Littlewood 1986), 'A Halifax Cider Jar' (Yorkshire Art Circus 1987), 'Into the Ashes' (Littlewood 1988) and 'Sky Burial' (Dangaroo 1988). He now lives in North Yorkshire where he works as a freelance writer, editor and creative writing tutor.

DOROTHY NIMMO writes: Born in Manchester, educated in York and Cambridge. An actress in London, mother-of-four in Geneva and Peterborough, returned to the North West in 1980 and began writing, encouraged by the writing groups in Lancaster and Kendal. Published A Woman's Work, (Brazen Voices, Lancaster 1984). Poems in Purple and Green anthology, Rivelin Grapheme Press 1985. Stories in First Fictions, (Faber 1986). Homewards (poems), Giant Steps (1987). Is completing an M.A. in creative writing at Lancaster University.

MICK NORTH was born in Lancaster in 1958, where he still lives. He has worked as Director of the Lancaster Literature Festival. His first pamphlet of poems 'Throp's Wife' was published by Jackson's Arm in 1986, the same year in which he received a major Gregory Award.

IRENE RAWNSLEY is an ex-teacher who now writes mainly for children. Her work has been mostly poetry; her first book 'Ask a Silly Question', poems for young children, was published by Methuen in July 1988. In September 1987 her poem-sequence 'Hiding Out' was broadcast by BBC Education. She takes her poems into schools and libraries as a visiting writer and also works with teachers to promote the writing and reading of poetry in schools. She has lived for the past five years in Settle, North Yorkshire, with her son.

NEIL ROBERTS writes: Born in Manchester 1946, grew up in Middlesex. Educated at Oriel Primary School, Hanworth, Latymer Upper School, Hammersmith and Clare College, Cambridge. Has taught English Literature at Sheffield University since 1970, and lives with his wife and two children in a former Primitive Methodist manse in the Peak District. Has published books on George Eliot and Ted Hughes, and numerous essays on modern literature as well as stories in Delta, Stand, Arts Council New Stories and Critical Quarterly.

PETER RYDE grew up in London, but has lived in South Lincolnshire since 1960. After winning a children's short story competition at the age of 11, he decided to be a novelist, but it didn't work out. Instead he became a History teacher, film maker, and technical journalist. Now retired, he works part-time as a film archivist. About three years ago, he suddenly found himself starting to write poetry and short stories; his poems have appeared in a number of magazines and anthologies, but he has not previously published any fiction.

VALERIE SMITH writes: I live in Harrogate, although I was born and grew up in West London. I am a part-time tutor in adult education, including the Open University; I teach mostly English and study skills, mostly in Leeds. This is a mid-life career change: I used to be a hospital biochemistry technician. I studied for a London University external degree while looking after my two small daughters (now grown up). I have been writing poetry for many years (runner-up, National Poetry Competition, 1978, winner, Cheltenham Festival/TLS 1987) and have recently started to work at short stories.

JOAN THORNTON writes: I was born in South Yorkshire but left the area at 19 and only returned eight years ago. I've had a variety of jobs from barmaid to company director and 10 years ago became a free-lance training consultant which has taken me to the United States, Europe and Japan. I've had short stories published by *Pan* and I co-edited a community history of Calderdale called *'It Were No Laughing Matter.'* I'm currently editing a collection of Barnsley short stories, co-writing a South Yorkshire soap opera and trying to finish a novel.

THERESA TOMLINSON spent her childhood on the North-East Coast of Yorkshire, and now lives with her husband and three children in Sheffield. After ten years of collecting rejection-slips she has recently begun to get her stories accepted. *'The Flither Pickers'* was published by *Littlewood* in 1987, *'The Water Cat'*, a children's story, is to be published by *Julia Macrae* in 1988, and *'Summer Witches'* is due from the same publisher in 1989. Her interests are children's books, folklore, local history and women's history.

SUE WILSEA writes: Having acquired a degree in English from Hull University, I then spent ten years attempting to teach the subject in a local comprehensive before leaving the profession to write. However, I still teach part-time at Hull prison and in Further Education in order to provide the little luxuries in life (food, heating). I have had poems, articles and short stories in several small press publications and regional literary magazines and on local radio. My work was included in an anthology *'Pigs is Pigs'* (*Unwin / Hyman*) earlier this year and I have an article to be published shortly in *The Guardian*. I am assistant editor of *Inkshed* magazine and have just completed my first novel. Any other time is spent refamiliarising myself with husband and four children.

NANCY CLARE WYNNE writes: I had a well-heeled youth, my father being a Lord. War came. I joined the ATS, married a handsome young Lance Corporal and have lived happily ever afterwards. We have five daughters and one son, and eight grandchildren. We have lived in Blackpool since 1949, running every imaginable business from Boarding House to Golf Driving Range. I was on the Town Council for thirty-one years. We were the Mayor and Mayoress in 1972. I have had a few short stories published, and a number of poems in *Punch, She* and *Lancashire Life*.